THE SAVAGE TRAIL

THE SAVAGE TRAIL

JORY SHERMAN

THORNDIKE
CHIVERS

This Large Print edition is published by Thorndike Press, Waterville, Maine, USA and by BBC Audiobooks Ltd, Bath, England.

Thorndike Press, a part of Gale, Cengage Learning.

The text of this Large Print edition is unabridged.

Other aspects of the book may vary from the original edition.

Set in 16 pt. Plantin.

Printed on permanent paper.

LIBRARY OF CONGRESS CATALOGING-IN-PUBLICATION DATA

Sherman, Jory.
    The savage trail / by Jory Sherman.
        p. cm. — (Thorndike Press large print western)
    ISBN-13: 978-1-4104-1129-7 (alk. paper)
    ISBN-10: 1-4104-1129-X (alk. paper)
    1. Large type books. I. Title.
    PS3569.H43S28 2008
                                    813'.54—dc22   2008035368

BRITISH LIBRARY CATALOGUING-IN-PUBLICATION DATA AVAILABLE

Published in 2008 in the U.S. by arrangement with The Berkley Publishing Group, a member of Penguin Group (USA) Inc.
Published in 2009 in the U.K. by arrangement with The Berkley Publishing Group, a member of Penguin Group (USA) Inc.

U.K. Hardcover: 978 1 408 42173 4 (Chivers Large Print)
U.K. Softcover: 978 1 408 42174 1 (Camden Large Print)

Printed in the United States of America
1 2 3 4 5 6 7 12 11 10 09 08

For Diane and David Flack

1

John Savage couldn't shake it off. The stench of death was still in his nostrils, as strong and cloying as the day his parents, along with so many friends, were killed. Death cloaked him like an old, moth-eaten overcoat, heavy and musty. But these were men he had killed and the revulsion he felt now was no less than on that fateful day when Ollie Hobart and his men had come to the mining camp bent on robbery and slaughter.

"Too bad that damned Hobart got away," Ben Russell said, a slight quaver in his voice. "Was he one of them lyin' there dead, you could hang up that gun your pa left you."

"He's not the only one who got away. I don't see Army Mandrake here."

"That Dick Tanner ain't among the dead here, neither."

"Nope. He should be, the bastard."

John had just finished reloading the pistol

and it was back in its holster. Yes, Ollie Hobart had gotten away, along with that woman, Rosa. But John knew where they were headed. It was plain that Ben wanted him to quit chasing the man responsible for all those murders. He'd had his fill of bloodletting. So had he, for that matter, but he couldn't let Hobart get away with murder.

There were the smells of Rosa's Cantina in the room, too, the faint scents of whiskey, mezcal, tequila, beer, the stomach-wrenching stale odor of cigar and cigarette smoke that lingered in the air and in every nook and cranny, like egg-laden cobwebs.

John and Ben walked through the deserted cantina one last time. The body of Red Dillard, not much older than John, lay on its back staring sightlessly into eternity.

"Ollie killed him," Ben said. "His own man."

"Right between the eyes."

"What do you make of a man like Hobart, John?" Ben asked. He cut off a chunk of tobacco with his knife, stuffed it in his cheek.

"You can't figure a man like that. Born killer, I guess."

"Born, or made?"

"There you go again, Ben, making

8

judgments."

Ben held up both hands in mock surrender.

"I warn't judgin', John. Just is I wonder when the killin's goin' to stop, that's all."

"When Hobart is six feet under."

"You kill him, you got to kill Rosa, his woman. They're paired up like two spoons."

"I know, Ben. It don't bother me none."

"Christ, John, you're gettin' a heart hard as a damned rock."

"No harder than the one still beatin' in Hobart's chest."

"But to kill a woman, John," Ben said. "I don't know."

"My father told me once about his trip out West. He and my mother were in a wagon train, and most of the folks had dogs they brought with them from home. At night, they'd hear the coyotes howl and sometimes they got real close. He said the coyotes would send a bitch close to the wagons. The female was in heat. The male dogs put up a ruckus, and if one of 'em got loose and chased that bitch in heat, the other coyotes would pounce on him and tear him to pieces."

"Yeah? And so?"

"Every time a female coyote came near, they shot it and their dogs didn't chase after that bitch and get killed."

"Not the same thing," Ben said, a stubborn jut to his jaw.

"Something to keep in mind when you're talking about women, Ben. Women who run with a pack of wild dogs."

Ben shook his head and gave up.

John ignored him and walked on through the room for one last check of dead bodies.

"Let's get the hell out of here, Ben," John said, finally.

"Yeah. I seen enough dead here to last me the rest of my life."

John said nothing, but he was already thinking about Hobart, about making him pay for the murder of his parents and all those innocent miners.

"We'll pick up Hobart's trail directly," John said as the two men mounted their horses. I figure he's heading for Cheyenne. That tally with what you think?"

"Onliest way he can go," Ben said. "North, and Cheyenne would suit him about now. Rosa, too, I reckon."

"Yeah, he can't head back south. All of his men are dead, the ones who rode with him. Cheyenne it is."

"Ought to be easy to track. You already can read his sign."

That was true. John was a good tracker,

taught by his father, who could tell if a frog had sat on a lily pad or where a snake had crawled across dry rock.

He knew the tracks of Hobart's horse, had memorized the marks the shoes left, the nicks in the iron, where each was worn down on edges and heels.

John clucked to his horse, Gent, the Missouri-bred trotter, and gently nudged his flanks with the tips of his blunt rowels. He looked back, but Ben was still sitting his horse, not moving.

"Come on, Ben. What's holding you up?"

"Maybe we ought to sleep on this, Johnny," Ben said.

"No. We don't want to let Hobart get too far ahead of us. Come on."

"I don't know."

John reined up his horse and turned it around. He rode up to Ben.

"I'm going after Hobart, Ben. You want to stay in Denver, go on."

"You got to get over this, Johnny. You want revenge for what Hobart did to your folks, I know."

"My folks and everybody else up there. If we hadn't been in that cave, we'd be buzzard bait right alongside them."

"So you're bent on revenge, I reckon."

"I am."

11

"You know what they say about that, don't you?"

"About revenge?"

"Yeah. Revenge." Ben spat the word out as if he had bitten a caterpillar in half.

"No, I don't. And I don't care."

"Well, you better listen. If you take up the trail to get revenge, they say, you better dig two graves."

John said nothing. A sound startled him as he turned his horse.

"You hold it right there, sonny," boomed a loud voice from out of the shadows, "or I'll blow you plumb off that horse."

"What the hell?" Ben said.

"You, too, you old galoot. Step down from them horses, the both of you. And keep your hands high."

John felt a cold chill as three men stepped out of the shadows, the snouts of their rifles glistening in the moonlight, black and deadly.

Ben swallowed hard and felt the hackles on the back of his neck stiffen and bristle as if spiders were crawling up his spine.

The sound of the rifles all cocking at once made both men sweat as they lifted their hands. The metallic snicks lingered on the air like faint crackles of lightning.

2

Oliver Hobart would have ridden his dun horse into the ground if Rosa Delgado hadn't stopped him. She let out a shrill cry, followed by a stream of invective in Spanish that was like a scalding liquid poured into his ears.

"Para, cabrón, tu hijo de mala leche, tu diablo de chingadero, salvaje pendejo sin juevos, tu hijo de fea puta."

Ollie hauled in hard on the reins. The dun skidded to a stop, fighting the bit. Ollie turned the horse's head and glared at Rosa Delgado's shadowed eyes. He had understood every filthy word and his anger boiled up in him until his neck swelled like a bull in the rut.

"What the hell, Rosa, you gone plumb loco?"

"You are killing the horses, Ollie, and me. My side hurts."

"Hell, we got to make tracks, lady."

13

"There is nobody following us. Look back. The lights of Denver are dim and far away."

Hobart looked up and saw the orange lights in the distance, tiny jack-o'-lanterns winking through the evening haze. He heaved a sigh.

"We're not far enough away, Rosa, even so. That Savage is like a dead cat. He keeps coming back with more lives."

"Are you afraid of him, Ollie?"

"Not him. That gun of his. Look what he's done to my men."

"He's just a man. His gun is not so special."

The horses were heaving, blowing the snot from their rubbery noses, their ribs expanding and contracting under their hides. They had not started to lather, but Hobart knew they needed rest after that long gallop.

"It's special the way that bastard uses it," he said. "I'd like to own such a gun. And maybe, by damn, I will, one of these days."

"We could wait and hide along the road," she said, "shoot them as they come by. It's just Savage and that old man."

"We might do that. Ever try to shoot something in the dark? Your eyes play tricks on you. You shoot either high or low. If we missed Savage, he'd be on us like ugly on a bear."

"We could use the scatterguns," she said.

"Maybe. Still a big risk."

"I want to go back to my cantina."

"Your brother can take care of that, Rosa. But I'll tell you what. You can go on back there now, if you want. I got business in Fort Laramie and I'm ridin' on to Cheyenne."

"What business in Fort Laramie?"

"My business."

"You bastard. You never tell me anything."

"Maybe you don't want to know. I'm going to meet up with Army Mandrake there."

"That man. It's too bad he wasn't at the cantina. Maybe you'd be rid of him."

"Army is one of my best men."

"You mean he don't have no conscience." Ollie laughed.

"Maybe. He's not afraid of nobody and he handles a knife better'n anyone I know. Army is a good man. A damned good man."

"He's a killer, *sin verguenza*."

"Ain't we all, though?" Ollie said with a wry laugh.

The horses were still breathing hard, blowing jets of steam from their nostrils that shone in the moonlight like miniature clouds floating across the face of the moon. There was no traffic on the Cheyenne road at that hour and it was quiet.

15

"If I go with you, Ollie, I want to know."

"Not yet. I got to keep some things to myself."

"Bastard," she said again.

He could almost feel her anger, but he didn't care if Rosa went with him or not. She had been someone to use back in Denver, but unless she could be of help to him now, she was just so much unnecessary baggage, just like those no-accounts who had gotten themselves killed back at the cantina. The West was full of dumb men like them. They had no trade, rode the owlhoot trail, and just drifted from one sorry place to another looking for an easy poke.

"Make up your mind, Rosa," Ollie said, reaching into his shirt pocket for a ready-made. He kept listening for hoofbeats, a sign that Savage and his partner were coming after him, but the quiet remained. He worked a cigarette out of the pack, put it between his lips. He was surprised when Rosa leaned over with a box of matches, struck one, and lit his cigarette. She did that sort of thing. She could be a warm woman on a cold night, but she had a jealous streak a yard wide and had her a temper. She was away from her home now and he didn't know how far he could trust her. Probably about as far as he could throw her horse, he thought.

"I don't have no pretty clothes, no paint for my lips, no underwear. I don't got nothing."

"I can buy you those things in Cheyenne."

"You got a lot of money, Ollie?"

"Enough."

"You said you had a lot of gold."

"I have money, I said. Just quit your damned bellyachin', Rosa. Or get the hell back to Denver. I don't need no whinin' woman with me."

"I thought you loved me, *querido.* You told me you loved me, eh?"

"Aw, stop that, Rosa. I love you, darlin'. I just got other things on my mind now."

He wanted to smack her across the mouth. But he realized that he needed her, too. She was a good shot, could ride as well as any man, and if it came to a showdown with Savage, he could use her, maybe, another way. Savage might think twice before shooting a woman, and if she was between him and Savage, that would give him a slight edge.

"Well, I don't want to just run like the rabbit and not have nothing."

"I'll take care of you, Rosa. And once Savage is six feet under, you can go back to your cantina. I'll go with you. We can have a

17

good life, you and me."

"Promise?" she said.

"I promise," he lied. "We'll lay over at Fort Collins for a time, buy some fresh horses."

"And buy me some new clothes there?"

"In Cheyenne, maybe. I don't want to linger."

"My clothes will fall off by the time we get to Cheyenne. I am already smelling."

"You smell just fine to me, Rosa. It won't hurt you none to wait until we get to Cheyenne."

"Yes, it will," she said.

"Daylight is my enemy right now. We'll rest up in Fort Collins, ride out before daybreak."

"You are a bastard, Ollie. You are without shame."

He didn't argue with her. He was, in fact, a bastard. He carried the name Hobart, but had no idea who his real father was. What's more, Ollie didn't care. He had always told his mother that if he ever ran into his father, he'd kill him.

After the horses were rested, and Rosa's side stopped hurting, they rode on toward Cheyenne over the road dappled in moonlight, the Rockies looming dark to the west of them, the Platte a shining ribbon of silver marking their way.

18

3

Ben dismounted first, holding one arm up, then the other, as he stepped from the stirrup.

"You just hold it right there, old-timer," the voice from the shadows said. "Now, sonny, you step down real easy."

John got down from his horse, stood by its side with both hands in the air.

Three men emerged from the darkness, their rifles still pointed at John and Ben.

John saw the flash of a silver star on one of the men's vests.

"That him?" one of the men said. He stepped up close to John. He, too, wore a badge on his vest.

"Naw. Never seen this one before."

The man in front, obviously the one in charge, stepped up beside the other deputy and scanned John's face.

"Charlie, you go inside. Take Rob with you. See if Mandrake's in there."

"Right, Bill," Charlie said. He and the other men went into the cantina.

"I'm Sheriff Bill Dorsett, feller. You part of that gang?" Dorsett looked John square in the eyes, as if looking for the slightest flicker.

"No," John said. "And Mandrake's not in there."

"What about a man named Dick Tanner?"

John shook his head.

"There's been a shooting here," Dorsett said. "You any part of that?"

"The men you named, and those inside, murdered my parents and a bunch of miners. They tried to kill me and my friend there."

"You the one with the pretty gun?"

"I'm John Savage."

"I heard about you. Hell, everybody in Denver has. A man named Hobart robbed some miners and killed them all."

"Same bunch," John said.

Dorsett turned to Ben.

"You back him on that? Who're you?"

"I'm Ben Russell. Yep. We was up in a mine when these jaspers come and shot all our friends, his folks, stole our pokes."

The two deputies, Charlie Haskell and Rob Emmons, came back outside.

"They's some dead men in there, Bill,"

Charlie said. "Didn't see Mandrake ner Tanner. Place is plumb empty. Lamps still burnin' and all."

"It's right spooky in there," Rob said, his voice quavering slightly.

"Put your hands down," Sheriff Dorsett said. "Maybe we can sort all this out. Can I take a look at that pistol of your'n I been hearing about?"

"I don't like to pass it around," John said.

"Just want to say I seen it," Dorsett said. "C'mon. I'll give it right back."

"Maybe if you all take your rifles off of us," John said.

"Oh yeah. Charlie, Rob. Put 'em away."

John slid his pistol from its holster, handed it butt first to Dorsett, who handed his rifle to Charlie.

Dorsett held the pistol up, then turned it over and over. He squinted to read the legend engraved on the barrel, holding the gun so that it caught the light from the lamps inside Rosa's Cantina.

The inlays shot silver lances from the blue-black barrel, grips, and receiver, like tiny searchlights.

"Beautiful," Dorsett said. "What's that mean, that writing on the barrel. Spanish, ain't it? My Spanish ain't none too good."

"Ni me saques sin razon, ni me quardes sin

21

honor," John said from memory. "It means, 'neither draw me without reason, nor keep me without honor.' "

The two deputies crowded close to examine the pistol in the sheriff's hand. John licked his lips, dry from worry over his pistol. He was ready to snatch it back if it went any farther from where it was in Dorsett's hand.

"Mighty nice sentiment," Dorsett said.

"I hold to it," John said. "May I have my pistol back, Sheriff?"

"Sure. I guess it's okay." Dorsett handed the pistol back to John the same way, butt first. John slipped it back in his holster, stepped back a pace.

"What did Mandrake do that's got you looking for him?" John asked.

"He cut a man's throat. We know he's in with Oliver Hobart. We got wanted flyers on the whole damned bunch. Those men inside the cantina. They Hobart's men?"

"Yes," John said.

"Cutthroats, just like Mandrake," Ben said.

The sheriff turned and looked at Ben.

"You didn't get 'em all. Hobart wasn't in there, or Charlie would have told me. We got a good description of him, most of the ones who run with him."

22

"Nope, Hobart slipped out with Rosa herself."

"We had an eye on her, too. I reckon we didn't watch her close enough."

"Fact is," Charlie said, "we didn't even know Hobart and his gang were in Denver till Mandrake kilt Bernie Robbins over at the Brown Palace this afternoon."

"There'll be hell to pay over this," Dorsett said, his jaw tightening. The other two deputies wore grim looks on their faces.

"I don't know the man," John said. "Who was Bernie Robbins?"

"Territorial marshal," Dorsett said. "We knew him. Good man. Mandrake near cut his head off with a big bowie knife. Got him from behind, while Tanner pinned Bernie's arms. Slicker'n winter snot, the bastards."

"Why?" John asked. "Was this Bernie on to Hobart, huntin' him?"

"We don't know. Bernie rode down from Laramie where he's been working on a case. Said he was near to calling in the U.S. Army and closing it out. Said he got a telegram from somebody down here who could fill in all the missing pieces."

"You think Hobart sent the telegram?"

"It sure fooled Bernie. He was hoppin' glad that he could solve his case."

Ben moved closer. The lights from the

23

cantina threaded his beard, glistened in the depths of his eyes like candle flames.

"What kind of case was this U.S. marshal on?" he asked.

"Seems like somebody up in Laramie's been smuggling in a lot of guns, Henrys and Winchesters, ammunition. And a whole lot of Mexicans come up from down south, then disappeared along with all them guns."

"Doesn't make much sense to me," Ben said.

"Not to anybody else, neither," Dorsett said. "But Bernie said it looked like somebody was going to start a war, and the law up there got worried about the Arapaho, Southern Cheyenne, even the Sioux, breakin' loose and goin' on the warpath. Mighty puzzlin', you ask me."

"So the marshal doesn't know where the guns went or why all those Mexicans disappeared," John said.

"Nope. He was still working on the case. But he said he'd heard the name Hobart more'n once and then that telegram come and said much the same thing. That Hobart was here and some of his men wanted out of the deal and would talk to him. Hobart set him up, and Mandrake killed him."

"Must be something big," John said. "But why would Hobart want the Indians to go

24

on the warpath?"

"Bernie didn't think that was it. He said he thought Hobart was putting together his own private army for some damned reason."

"Well, you can bet there's money stuck to that reason," John said.

"I sent a telegram off to Washington this afternoon. The government's going to have to send somebody up here to take up where Bernie left off. Going to take some time, probably. That's why I was hoping we'd find Hobart here. Maybe meeting up with Mandrake and Tanner. Looks like they got clean away."

"Why don't you get a posse together and go after them?" John asked.

"They've got too much of a head start on me. By the time I rounded up enough good men to chase after Hobart, he'd be in Cheyenne, I reckon. 'Sides, I got to tell my sister about Bernie."

"Your sister?" John shifted his weight. It seemed he had been standing in one spot for hours and one of his feet was going to sleep.

"Bernie was going to marry my sister Nancy when this was all over. Now, I'll have to take her up to Laramie so she can pack up all her things he took up there with him."

"Yeah," Charlie said. "Bernie was going to

25

resign as a marshal and work for the sheriff in Laramie. Nancy was set on going up there to live."

John let out a breath.

"If you tell me where Bernie lived, maybe Ben and I can pack up your sister's things and freight them back here to you, Sheriff. Save you and Nancy a trip, maybe."

John was thinking that he might find out more about Hobart's scheme if he was able to look through the marshal's papers.

"Would you do that?" Dorsett said. "Save me a heap of trouble, for sure."

"Be glad to," John said.

"I'll tell you how to get to Bernie's place and give you my address where to ship the stuff. Hell, I'll pay you to do it."

John waved his hands at the sheriff.

"No, Sheriff. I'll take care of it."

"That's mighty good of you, Savage. And me and my men will take care of what happened here at Rosa's, so you don't have to worry none about that."

"What do you mean?"

"Oh, we'll make out a report that we followed Mandrake and Tanner out here and shot all them men dead in there."

"You mean you'll take credit for that?"

"Why, sure," Dorsett said.

"Then, Ben and I will ride off and follow

Hobart. Might catch him in Cheyenne."

"Might," Dorsett said. "Do us all a service if you did." He told John how to get to Bernie's place.

John looked at Dorsett. Shadows on the sheriff's jowly face made him look like a bulldog in the dim light. He was a stocky man with a belly that hung over his gunbelt like a sack of meal. The deputies were trimmer, leaner, probably because they did most of the work while the sheriff spent his time drinking beer and eating vittles.

"All right. Ben, you ready?"

"John, you ought not to . . ."

"Mount up," John said, knowing that Ben was going to try to talk him out of going after Hobart. But now John wanted to find him more than ever. Mandrake and Tanner, too. Such men were a scourge on the earth. Dangerous, mean, and lawless.

"Good luck to you, Savage," Dorsett said.

"You'll be hearing from me, Sheriff," John said as he hauled himself into the saddle. He and Ben raised their hands in farewell as they rode off into the night.

Ben started grumbling as soon as they were out of earshot of the sheriff and his deputies.

"John, this is too big for you. You ought to let the law take care of Hobart and his men."

"I ought to, Ben. But the law already tried and failed. Mandrake made a widow out of a woman who hadn't even gotten married yet."

"That don't make no sense."

"None of it does, Ben," John said, but now he saw a greater purpose in killing Hobart. Who knew how many lives he might save by wiping Hobart and his men off the face of the earth?

John's jaw hardened with determination.

And now, thanks to Sheriff Dorsett, he knew where Hobart was going. If he didn't find him in Cheyenne, they'd ride on to Laramie.

He had a mission and he was going to carry it out if it killed him.

4

Melvin Willis had not realized how rough the trail was when he had driven his wagon up to high ground the night before. Now, as he gazed down at the road, he realized why the mule was balking, standing motionless in the traces despite repeated lashes of the buggy whip on its rump.

"Use the quirt, Mel," Darlene said, "or we'll be up here all day." She sat next to her husband on the springboard seat, a folded fan in her lap. "It's going to get hot real quick and we've a long drive until we get to Fort Collins."

"I know, I know," Mel said. "The quirt won't do more'n make old Jubal that much ornerier. He's spooked, that's all, over what he's got to do. He'll step out directly."

"Pa," their son, Calvin, said from his perch on the wagon, "you want me to get down and hold out a carrot for Jubal?"

"No, Cal, just sit tight."

Mel flicked the whip once again. The thin lash flapped up dust and left a mark on Jubal's rump. The mule didn't budge.

"Shit," Mel said.

"Mel," Darlene said. "Not around the boy."

"Damned mule. Haw, Jubal."

The mule switched its tail, stood staring down at the steep, rocky trail.

"I could give Jube a push," Cal said. His face bore a serious look. His father's eyes rolled in their sockets. Darlene sat there, twiddling with the folded fan. The sun crept up toward the eastern horizon, the sky filling with light. The trees and rocks around them stood out in stark relief as etched into a permanence that hadn't been there before.

"One more time," Mel said and swung his arm back. The whip made a crack with the force of his forward thrust. The lash smacked onto the mule's rump. Its hide rippled under the blow and the mule hunched its shoulders and jerked forward, pulling the traces taut.

"Now he's moving," Darlene said with a breath of relief pushing her words.

"Finally," Cal said, his eyes alight with eagerness.

Mel said nothing, but gripped the reins tight without pulling on them. He wanted the mule to keep moving, but braced himself in case Jubal lost his footing and began walking too fast.

"Hold on," Mel said to his wife and son. "Going to be tricky."

Darlene grabbed a side panel. Cal braced himself. The wagon rumbled over the rocks as the mule picked up speed. The wagon teetered from side to side as the wheels rolled over rocks. Mel heard a sound that froze his blood. He saw a rattlesnake coiled up next to a rock, its tail quivering. The mule saw it, too, and swerved to the left, off the path. Mel, Darlene, and Cal bounced up and down as the wagon rolled into brush and rocks. Mel pulled on the right rein, trying to steer Jubal back onto the rough-cut road.

Jubal didn't respond.

Instead, the mule began to buck and kick as sharp branches broke off bushes and jabbed him in the belly and flanks. He began to bellow his hoarse hee-haws. The wagon pitched and rolled like a ship on a storm-tossed ocean and careened down the hillside, out of control as the reins slipped from Mel's hands.

Near the bottom, the wagon jounced upward and came down hard. One wheel struck a large rock with a sickening crunch.

The wagon lurched to a halt, one end careening at a dizzying angle. There was a loud twanging sound as the iron rim broke and one end clanged against a stone. A spoke snapped and the right front wheel collapsed. Spokes loosened and tumbled to the ground like sticks of firewood.

Darlene screamed. She was thrown backward as the wagon jolted to a stop and teetered to the right, its axle jammed against a rock. She pitched forward and Mel had to reach out and grab her to keep her from falling into the traces behind the mule.

Cal was thrown backward, too, and lay sprawled on top of the trunks and carpetbags like a splayed scarecrow. His head had slammed into the tailgate, knocking him nearly senseless. A large knot began to grow atop his head like some angry red egg. His head throbbed and his eyes wouldn't focus for several seconds.

Mel swore.

Jubal stood there, tangled in the traces, as docile as a tame jackrabbit, his large ears twitching, his tail switching slowly back and forth to swat the deer flies. Hoofbeats sounded down on the main road. Darlene was breathing hard, holding on to him, her nails digging through his shirt and into the flesh on his back. Her eyes were shut tight as she cowered in her husband's arms, her hands trembling, her arms quivering against his sides like frog legs in a hot fry pan.

Mel saw two riders out of the corner of his eye and they were heading straight toward them from the south.

"Darlene," Mel said. "Are you hurt?"

"I-I don't know," she said. "I don't think so."

"Couple of riders. Maybe they can help us fix that wheel."

"You've got tools, Mel. I can help you. So can Cal. Cal, where are you? Mel, is he all right?"

Mel looked over his shoulder. Cal was still lying on his back, spread-eagled. Still. A sudden spasm of fear gripped Mel's throat.

"Cal?" Darlene said, a note of fear in her voice, a voice teetering on the edge of hysteria. She untangled herself from her husband's arms and tried to sit up. Gravity held her off center of the seat.

"I think he got knocked out," Mel rasped, his voice husky in a dry throat.

"For God's sake, Mel, find out," Darlene screeched, her voice rising to a high pitch just short of a scream.

Mel climbed into the wagon, crawled up beside his son. Cal's eyes were closed. His face was wan, so drained of color his complexion reminded Mel of men released from prison after many years. He gently shook his son, spoke his name.

"Cal, Cal, you wake up, hear?"

Cal's eyelashes quivered as if he was trying to open the lids. Mel patted one cheek, put a hand on his shoulder, and shook him again.

"Cal, wake up, boy."

Darlene struggled on the seat trying to crawl into the wagon.

"Is he — Mel, is he . . . ?"

"No, he's not dead. Just sit tight, Darlene."

The riders came closer, but they were still some distance away. Darlene looked down toward them, shading her eyes with the flat of her hand.

"Knocked cold, I reckon," Mel said, more to himself than to Darlene. He slid an arm under Cal's back, just below the shoulder blades, and hefted him almost to a sitting position.

"Cal, boy, you got to come out of it," Mel said almost in a whisper. "Your pants are on fire."

"Huh — wha?" Cal's eyes opened and he stared up at his father.

Mel smiled.

"I said wake up." He saw the lump on

34

Cal's head, touched it gingerly.

Cal winced and let out a cry.

"Ouch."

"Got you a pretty fair lump on your noggin, son," Mel said.

"I reckon. Pa, I don't feel so good."

"You'll be all right. Just take it easy. Lie back down until your head stops spinnin'."

"It ain't spinnin'. It's throbbing." Cal reached up and felt the knot on his head.

"Is it bleeding?" he asked his father.

"Nope, not so's I can see. You just got a crack on the head. Ma can put a poultice on it by-and-by and the swellin' will go down."

"Feels like an old darnin' egg," Cal said with a wince that brought a crinkle to his lips. Not quite a smile, but almost.

Mel looked at the riders again. They were leaving the road, heading up the woodcutter's trail. He could not see their faces. The rising sun was behind them. He raised a hand in a welcome wave. Neither rider responded.

That's when Mel's blood began to run cold.

"Darlene," he said. "You better come back here and take care of Cal."

Darlene stiffened at the tone of her husband's voice. There was an edge to it, as if

35

he was concealing something, anger perhaps, worry, or . . . fear.

"Is Cal all right?" she said.

"Those riders. I don't like the looks of
them. You come back here and I'll get my
rifle."

"Mel, don't start trouble now," she said.

"I ain't. I just don't like the looks of them
two."

"Oh, you're suspicious of everybody.
They're probably riding up here to help us."

"Yeah. Maybe." But that edge was still
there in his voice.

Darlene climbed into the wagon, her skirts
hindering her, the cloth catching on the
wood. She reached down and pulled herself
free, then crabbed back to sit beside Cal.
She looked at the two riders. Their faces
were in shadow and one of them, the smaller
one, didn't look right.

"Mel, I think it's a man and a woman,"
she said.

He slipped his arms from under Cal's
back as Darlene reached for her son.

"I'm all right, Ma," Cal said. "Just got me
a headache and I feel a mite groggy."

"You just lie still for a minute, Cal," she
said. "Your pa's . . ."

"I know what he's going to do. He's going
to get the rifle. Just in case."

"Hush now. Those people mean us no harm," she said.

But there was a note of doubt in her voice, a querulous pitch to it that slipped into Cal's senses like an overheard whisper from another room. His mother was worried. His father was worried. That was disturbing enough, but when he looked at the two riders approaching, he felt his skin crawl. One was a tall man on a tall horse. The other was short, with large breasts and a skirt that draped down over her left stirrup. A woman, for sure. But she wore a gunbelt and he could see the butt of a pistol protruding from her holster.

Mel scrambled back into the seat. He bent over to retrieve the rifle underneath.

"Mister, you better be looking for a hammer or saw under there," the man on the tall horse said.

Mel looked up.

"Huh?" he said.

" 'Cause if you pull up anything else from underneath that seat, it'll be the last thing you do."

There was no mistaking the warning in the man's voice.

Mel raised up and shaded his eyes from the sun.

He still couldn't see their faces. But he

saw that one was a woman, and she was wearing a pistol. Rifles jutted from their scabbards.

They were not ordinary folks, Mel decided.

Not at all ordinary.

In fact, he thought, as he held his breath, they had suddenly turned dangerous.

He opened his mouth to say something, but his throat was frozen, dry as dust.

The mule brayed and shook its head.

A cloud drifted over the sun and blanketed them all in shade.

Mel saw the man's face then, and the glint of his eyes.

That's when the fear paralyzed him, turned his body and his heart to ice-cold stone.

5

Mel saw the look on the tall man's face and his own eyes watered. For a split second, Mel thought there was a pane of glass in front of his face and that something horrible was clawing to get at him. He heard a gasp from behind him and knew it was Darlene.

Then Cal spoke in a loud whisper. "Ma, I peed my pants. I'm scared."

"Shhh," Darlene said, clutching her son tightly to her breast. Both of them stared at the man on the tall horse, not at the woman riding with him.

The man spoke. "Hand over your poke," he said.

"What?" Mel said.

"You got any cash on you? Gold? Silver? Greenbacks?"

"I ain't got much."

"Hand it over. Right quick."

"You ain't goin' to shoot?"

"That depends," Hobart said.

"On what?"

"On how quick you hand me your poke."

"Well, I ain't got none on me. I mean, not in my pockets." Mel turned around and looked at Darlene. She saw the fear shimmering in his eyes like liquid shadows. "Hand me that wooden box where we keep the money," he said.

"But Mel, that's all the money we got."

"Lady, you better get that box and there better be nothing in it but gold, silver, and paper."

"I'll get it, Ma," Cal said.

"Sonny, you just shut your mouth and sit right still," Hobart said.

"Yes, sir."

Darlene released her grip on her son and rummaged through the blankets covering the goods in the wagon. She picked up a small wooden box and leaned toward Mel.

"Here," she said. "God, Mel, what are we goin' to do with no money?"

"Don't you worry none," he said, his voice quavery as a calm Louisiana lake trembling under the ripples of a cottonmouth's wake. "We'll make it up some way."

"Your man's right," Hobart said. "Now hand it over, Pilgrim."

Hobart rode in close, stretched out a hand.

That's when Mel made a very stupid decision.

He dropped the box onto the floor of the wagon, ducked down, and reached under the seat for his rifle. He grabbed it with one hand, jerked it toward him. He saw a flash of movement out of the corner of his eye.

Hobart's hand streaked downward toward the butt of his pistol.

Darlene and Cal saw a blur of flesh that was Hobart's hand. The movement was so quick, the shock to them so great, their expressions did not change.

"Bad idea," Hobart growled as his pistol cleared the holster. His thumb pressed the hammer down so that the pistol was cocked when it came level, its front sight blade lined up on Mel's body. Hobart squeezed the trigger, just a touch was all that it took, and the pistol barked, spat lead and flame from the muzzle.

The bullet struck Mel just under the right armpit. The impact of the .45-caliber lead ball, traveling at around 900 feet per second, slammed him into the seat, cracking the ribs on the other side. The exiting lead ripped out more of his rib cage and blood spurted from the hole in his side and flowed onto the seat bed.

Darlene screamed.

Cal gasped and tears welled up in his eyes.

Darlene stood up, started to rush to Mel. Her son grabbed at her to pull her back down.

Rosa Delgado, who rode with Hobart, drew her pistol and cocked it.

"Mel, Mel," Darlene said, her voice full of anguish. Tears flooded her face as she jerked away from Cal.

She took one step toward her husband when Hobart fired again. There was the slow curl of a smile on his face when he fired his pistol. Darlene didn't see it, but Cal did. He cringed and squeezed his eyes shut when the Colt exploded. When he saw his mother's body jerk as the bullet struck her in the chest, his face contorted with rage.

He stood up and started rushing toward his mother.

Rosa calmly raised her pistol, sighted down the barrel, and squeezed the trigger. Her shot struck Cal in the throat, blowing out his Adam's apple, ripping through to his spine. The young man twisted his body in a macabre dance and his eyes rolled back in their sockets. Blood spurted from the hole in his neck. Fragments of splintered bone flew out from his broken backbone and his body turned rigid as it fell, a foot short of where his mother's twitching and bleeding body lay.

"Good shot, Rosa," Hobart said.

Rosa smiled. She held her pistol close to her as smoke curled from the barrel. She blew the smoke into wisps that glided into shreds and disappeared.

The smell of gunpowder hung in the air as both Rosa and Hobart holstered their pistols.

Hobart rode up close to the side of the wagon. He reached down and snatched up the box that Mel had dropped. He pulled on the latch, opened the lid.

He reached in and fished out a pile of greenbacks. He counted them and folded them, stuck them into his shirt pocket.

"Two hundred," he said. He scooped out the gold and silver coins and stuffed them into his pants pocket, then threw the opened box on the ground. It made a hollow clatter as it struck a rock and rolled over, forming a small wooden tent.

"Anything in the wagon you want, Rosa?" Hobart said.

"I'd like that mule, but we cannot take him."

"No."

"Then, let us go before someone sees us here."

She turned her horse and started back down toward the road. She pulled a fresh cartridge from her gunbelt, drew her pistol again, and set it to half cock. She opened the gate and rolled the cylinder until the spent cartridge appeared. She pushed the ejection rod and the empty hull fell out. She slipped a new cartridge in the chamber, closed the gate, and holstered her pistol, a Smith & Wesson .38 with pearl handles.

Darlene wheezed, blood spraying from her mouth. Hobart let out a breath, shook his head, and turned his horse to follow Rosa down the hillside. The mule brayed at them and then was silent.

"Were you going to kill them when you rode up there?" Rosa asked.

"I sure wasn't going to talk that jasper out of his poke."

"Are you going to give me half of the money you took from him?"

"No, Rosa. A third, for the boy."

"You are a bastard, Ollie. You know that."

"I know it," he said.

The South Platte was a ribbon of silver in the glaring sunlight. A hawk prowled the sky above it, sailing on an invisible current, its head moving slowly from side to side, eyes looking for any small movement. A pair of blackbirds rose from the grasses and gave chase, ragging at the hawk's tail, diving and darting, batting their wings, avoiding the raptor's talons.

Darlene turned over on her side, saw her son's body so near she could reach out and touch him if she had the strength. The pain drove her down into herself as if a huge nail had been hammered through her chest. She could not move, but the blood was starting to clot. Every breath was a struggle, and there was fire in her lungs. One of them was slowly filling up with blood, a slow seep that she could not feel. Her eyes closed and she concentrated on life, not death.

But she could feel it coming, see its dark shape on the inside of her eyelids, feel it envelop her with soft, warm arms.

6

Dynamite didn't like early morning any more than Ben, his rider, did. Ever since John and Ben had left Fort Collins, well above sunup, Dynamite had been exploding.

"You might have grit in your saddle blanket," John said right after Dynamite had tried to buck Ben off for the third time, fishtailing and snorting, coming down stiff-legged as if his legs were made out of broomsticks.

"No, I shook that blanket out, whopped it against the stall and everything else this mornin', John. Dynamite's just feelin' his oats."

"What'd you do, put chili peppers in his bin?"

"No, but oats is like fire to this horse. He gets some in his belly and old Dynamite's fuses start hissing. He'll settle down after he gets tired of trying to pitch me into the middle of next week."

John laughed.

The sun was still basking in the darkness before dawn when they rode through LaPorte, north of Fort Collins, where the Cache la Poudre streams into the South Platte. A lamp burned in the trading post, but there were no signs of life. The prairie lay to the east of them, the Rocky Mountains to the right, all in shadow like some deserted landscape. They had spent the night in Fort Collins because John couldn't track at night and both men were exhausted after their ordeal in Denver. John knew they had little chance of catching up with Hobart and he accepted that.

Now the eastern horizon began to pale. The light ate up the stars as it spread, and the sky turned a pale blue with not even the ghost of the moon as a reminder that there had been a night.

The sun rose above the horizon and drenched them with warmth. The snowy mountain peaks glistened like majestic monuments, so white John could not look at them for long. The chill seeped out of their bones. Dynamite had settled down and was trying to keep up with Gent's ground-eating easy gait. To John, it was like sitting in a rocking chair riding that Missouri trotter. It made him feel close to his dead father, too, for Gent had been his pa's horse.

They both heard the reports shortly after the sun had cleared the horizon.

"Pistols, I think," John said.

"Hard to tell. So far away," Ben said.

Then, they heard two more shots.

"Something's up," Ben said. "And it ain't good. Nobody I know goes huntin' with a pistol."

"Two shots from the same gun. One was from a smaller caliber. Thirty-eight, maybe."

"That third shot did sound a little funny."

"Stay on the quick, Ben."

They hadn't seen a soul on the Cheyenne road all morning. Now it seemed as if there might be trouble ahead.

A few moments later, a hawk flew down the South Platte, throwing its winged shadow on the hillside. A pair of blackbirds broke off and flew back the other way. The hawk *scree-screed* and veered away from them with just an incline of its wings, banking toward the foothills, its tail lifting and tilting as well.

John listened, but heard no more shots. Not so much as a hoofbeat or a yell.

In fact, he thought, it was ominously quiet. A half hour later, he saw something in the distance, an animal of some sort.

"I see it, too," Ben said, as if reading Savage's thought.

"It's not a deer," John said, although he was not sure.

"Could be a mulie. Or an elk, maybe."

"Down this low? Not an elk. Unless something chased it there."

"Horse?" Ben said.

"Maybe. So much brush up there, it's hard to tell."

They rode closer. It was eerily quiet and John felt uneasy.

"You ride out on the plain, Ben," Savage said. "I'll come up on this flank. Might be a bushwhacker lying in wait up there. It's just too damned quiet."

"I'll make a wide circle," Ben said.

The animal had disappeared. Either it was feeding and had lowered its head, or it had lain down, John thought. He crossed the river and urged Gent up the slope. If it was a deer or elk, he reasoned, it would soon catch his wind and bolt out of the brush. If so, he would see it plain. But as Gent scrambled for footing and he tested the wind, the animal became even more enigmatic. Still no sign of it, but he did see the trace of a road higher up, stretching to the top of a hill and beyond.

He looked down, across the river, and saw

Ben cutting his circle. By his reckoning, Ben ought to be coming close to where he would be opposite the place where they had seen the unidentified animal. John cut toward the road, figuring he was above the spot where they had seen the long ears and head of whatever it was on that brushy slope.

Something made John begin to tighten up inside. Some familiar memory circled his mind, triggered by the morning sunshine, the smell of steamed dew rising in the air, the aroma of something else he couldn't quite define. As he approached the animal, it lifted its head and he saw what it was: a mule. But that did not dispel John's uneasiness. The mule appeared to be tied or in harness. It was out of place, he knew that, and his senses prickled as if ice water had been poured down his back.

He rode closer, cautious, one hand resting on the stock of his rifle, ready to jerk it from its scabbard. His boots were poised to jab the rowels of his spurs into Gent's flanks and his left hand gripped the reins, ready to pull the bit tight in his horse's mouth and twist him into a tight turn away from danger.

Then John saw a flap of colored material, something pale blue, like chambray, maybe, such as might be part of a man's shirt.

Closer still, and he saw the outline of a wagon, bundles of clothes inside, a lump on the seat, a shining on something black, like hair.

His stomach knotted up as Gent's forelegs brought him onto a small knoll above the wagon. There, John saw what he hadn't been seeing, what he hadn't wanted to see, and out of the corners of his eyes, a rough, crude road that might have been hacked out by miners or woodcutters. And in the wagon, he saw lifeless bodies, bodies that flooded his brain with memories of the mining camp and the slaughter he and Ben had witnessed on just such a morning.

Dread crept into John's mind as he rode closer, forcing himself to look at what he knew he had to see. The lump on the front seat was a man. He was slumped over, unmoving, obviously dead. In the back, he saw a young man on his back, his throat torn away, replaced by a grisly crimson flower that was turning black. Between the boy and the man was a woman, her black hair shining like a crow's wing, glinting a shimmering jet obsidian in the sun, almost like a vibrant energy that set his nerves on edge. A wave of sadness washed over John like the tide that had gripped him when he saw the murdered body of his mother. No woman should have to die like that, he thought, so young, with hair like that, like a delicate Spanish fan made of black silk.

He looked away, down at Ben, who had stopped his horse opposite the mule and wagon, and now was looking up at him. John raised his hand and beckoned for him to ride up, not just sit there on Dynamite, gape-mouthed and puzzling over something neither of them would ever understand.

A slight breeze tugged at the man's shirt and that was the hardest part for John. Seeing his clothes like that, encasing his dead body, and the boy's hair. Invisible fingers of air tousling it. He choked at the sight. Something rose up in his throat and stuck there. And he thought about the young men in the mining camp, their bloody bodies strewn everywhere like drowned sailors floated to shore from a shipwreck, all lifeless, gone forever, but their voices still sounding in his ears. It was like that, seeing the three people in the wagon, all dead, their lives snatched from them and only their clothing and their bodies to mark their passing, their abrupt stop on a desolate hillside in the shadow of the Rockies.

John dismounted and tied Gent to a rear wagon wheel, then walked over to where the woman lay. The boy was clearly dead, and so was the man, but the woman was lying on her side and he could not see her face. It appeared to him that she had been reaching backward for the young man, who was most likely her son. He leaned over and touched the woman's chin, lifting it gently.

She let out a low moan. The sound startled John and he felt a rippling chill on the back of his neck as the small hairs stiffened and goose bumps crawled up both of his arms.

Gently, John slid an arm under her shoulder blades and turned her over, so that he could see her face, the front of her dress. He saw the blood on her blouse and felt a sticky wetness somewhere on her back.

He leaned down and put an ear to her mouth. There was a faint warm seep of air through her lips.

"You're alive," he said softly.

Her eyes were closed. Then they opened and stared up at him. They were a frosty blue.

"Yes," she said, so low and soft he barely heard her.

"You're hurt bad, ma'am."

"Ollie," she said.

"What? Did you say 'Ollie'? Is he the man who shot you?"

"Yesssss," she hissed, as if she could not stop the breath or did not want to stop it.

John heard the ring of a horseshoe on stone, heard the rustle of brush. He turned and saw Ben riding up. He was no more than ten yards from the mule.

"What you got there, John?"

"A woman. She's still alive. Just barely."

He turned back to the woman, spoke to her.

"I-I'll try to help you," he said.

Her eyes were closed and when he leaned down again, he could not detect her breathing. He put a finger on one of her eyelids and pried it open.

Ben rode alongside and looked down at the ground. He saw the open box. It was empty.

John looked at him, a sadness etching lines in his face.

"She — she's gone," he said. "Not breathing."

"Them others dead, too?" Ben asked, his voice just above a whisper.

John nodded. That lump was back in his throat again. Choking him.

"Mighty sorry sight," Ben said.

"She said Ollie shot her. In the chest."

Ben moved closer and peered at the woman. He could see the bullet hole in her chest.

John looked at her again, saw the trickle

of blood that had stopped oozing from the corner of her mouth.

He hadn't noticed it before. It might have come out with her last breath, he thought.

John sagged as if all his energy had gone out of him. He slumped there on the seat, next to the dead man, shook his head.

"It don't get no easier, Johnny, does it?" Ben said.

"Shut up, Ben. Just shut up for a minute."

It seemed as if there was a sigh in the wind that rushed over him, stirred the brim of his hat, touched the back of his neck, and blew on the sweat stain darkening the back of his shirt. The lump in his throat softened as tears spilled unbidden from his eyes and coursed down his cheeks.

Ben took off his hat, held it over his heart.

John did the same.

There was only silence as the breeze suddenly went slack and vanished under the mindless glare of the sun.

7

Ben stepped out of the saddle in a groaning whine of leather, tied his horse to a wagon wheel with sweat-slippery reins, and picked up the empty wooden box. He smelled the inside, sniffing to pick up any vagrant scents. He was thinking about candy, cigars, or the fragrance of baked flour in biscuits.

"Not a food box," he said aloud. "Cash box, maybe. Has that funny smell, like paper money."

John said nothing, his throat wound tight as if it had been coated with alum. His eyes closed up tight as fists as he fought back tears.

Ben looked at him, realizing John had gone to an island only he knew, some stark place in his heart where grief and sadness, remembrance, perhaps, were his only companions. He set the empty box in the rear of the wagon. Then he looked at the young man, the youth with the mangled throat, a throat that looked as if it had been clawed apart by some taloned beast with long hair or dusty feathers, one out of storybooks or mythical tales first told in ancient castle dungeons on nights so black a man couldn't see his hand in front of his face.

"All dead?" Ben sniffled, feeling his own throat tighten up as if it had been suddenly encased in a vise made of the coldest iron.

"Yeah."

"It's like looking at eternity, ain't it, John? Like starin' down into a bottomless well."

"I don't know what you mean, Ben."

"They've gone on from this place. God only knows where they are now. But, wherever they be, it's for the rest of eternity."

"Yeah. I guess I never looked at it that way." Even now, the thought was beyond comprehension, like a distance you can't measure, some endless dark sea.

"Any idea of who they were?"

"Why don't you start trying to find out. I'll go through the man's pockets, you check the boy's. There has to be something in the wagon that will tell us who they are."

"I reckon," Ben said.

"Then, we'll bury them. Cut that mule loose first chance."

"I'll do 'er," Ben said.

John steeled himself to go through the

pockets of the dead man on the seat. He didn't find much. There was a sack of tobacco and rolling papers, a box of wooden matches, a few coins, all of which he put back. The boy had nothing in his pockets. In the wagon itself, he found a carpetbag belonging to the woman. It had a number of items in it, including a comb, a small mirror, a tin of rouge, but most important, there was a letter that seemed recent, since the paper was still crisp and the ink strong and distinct.

Dear Darlene and Mel,
  Be sure and write me when you get settled in Fort Collins. It was sure good to see you two over the winter and young Calvin. He sure has grown. I will take good care of Sis. She ain't no trouble.
                    Your loving brother, Jess.

The letter was addressed to Melvin and Darlene Willis c/o General Delivery, Cheyenne, Wyoming. The return address was: Jesse Malone, 142 Locust Street, Fort Laramie, Wyoming.

John folded the letter and put it in his shirt pocket.

The people in the wagon, he reasoned, must be Darlene, Calvin, and Melvin. Jesse must be Darlene's brother, or a cousin, maybe. When they got to Fort Laramie, he vowed silently to look up the man and tell him what had happened to his kin. Maybe he would know something about the goings-on in Fort Laramie that involved Ollie Hobart.

He heard the mule braying and then a whack, saw it run down to the river and wade across to the road. It turned south, trotted a few yards, then stopped in its tracks.

"Wonder where he'll go," Ben said.

"I thought he might turn north and go back to where he came from. Cheyenne."

"You know he come from Cheyenne, Johnny?"

"That's where these folks have been staying for a spell. Before that they were in Fort Laramie."

"And how do you know all that?"

John patted the bulge in his shirt pocket.

"I got a letter written to them."

"Is there a shovel in that wagon?" Ben said.

A few minutes later, John handed Ben a shovel. He found a spade, too, and both set to digging the graves on the softest, least rocky part of the hillside. When they finished, they were drenched with sweat, their shirts black with it, their arms streaked with it, their mouths tasting of salty brine. They wrapped the bodies in blankets, carried them to the single scooped-out patch of earth that would serve as a grave. They lay the bodies in the ground with reverence and began covering them up. John put Darlene's carpetbag in the grave with her.

"You going to say a few words, John?" Ben asked when they had finished covering the graves with dirt and rocks.

"Not out loud."

"Well, we ought to say somethin'."

"You say it, then."

Ben took off his hat. So did John.

"Lord," Ben said, "we give these kind folks back to the earth. Dust unto dust. You take 'em into Heaven with you, you see fittin'. Amen."

John put his hat back on.

"That was a real fine prayer, Ben."

"Liked to not have finished it. Got me a lump in my throat."

"I know what you mean," John said. "Let's light out, let our sweat dry out some."

The two men rode away without a backward glance.

"They couldn't have had much," John said, an hour's ride up the trail.

"Huh?" Ben said. "What're you talkin' about?"

"Those people Hobart killed back there."

"No, I reckon not."

"He murdered three people. For money. What kind of man does that?"

"A bad man, John."

"Hobart's more than bad. He didn't have to kill them like that. In cold blood."

"They were witnesses, John. They saw his face. He had to kill 'em, I reckon."

John shook his head.

Ben could see that the killings had been bothering his friend. John hadn't said a word in better than an hour and now he was talking a blue streak. He had never talked much about his folks being killed, which had bothered Ben. A man hadn't ought to keep too much inside his self, he thought. It wasn't good for a man to carry too much weight on his shoulders. But John never got drunk, never cried in his sleep, and never let on how much grief he was packing in that young mind of his.

"No need to shoot the woman and boy," John said. "He could have just given them all a warning. Worse, I don't think Hobart needed what little money they probably had."

"No, I reckon not. He took us for a pretty

61

good chunk of gold. He ain't had time to spend it, and he's probably still got the shares of those you and me put six feet under."

"That's what bothers me, I guess. Hobart doesn't have a conscience. I think maybe he kills just for the fun of it."

"John, there's something I been meaning to tell you. Maybe now's the time."

John sat up stiff in the saddle and looked at Ben.

"What, Ben?"

"About Ollie Hobart."

"You been keeping something from me, Ben?"

"Afraid so, John."

"Why?"

"Just waitin' for the right time, I reckon."

John looked at his friend sharply, his eyes narrowing with suspicion. Ben hacked something up from his throat and spit it into the wind.

"And this is the right time, you figure," John said.

"As good as any. Your pa. He knew Ollie Hobart. Knowed him a long time back."

"What?"

"I think Dan was doin' his best to forget Ollie Hobart 'cause when they knowed each other, they was right young and Ollie . . .

well, he had a hankerin' for your ma, Clare. The both of them did, and there was bad blood atwixt 'em."

"Ollie Hobart was courtin' my ma?"

"Hell, he aimed to marry her. There was a hell of a row when Clare turned him down, said she was going to marry Dan Savage."

"I never heard anything about it."

"No, I reckon not."

"How come you know about it, Ben?"

"I was tradin' horse, twixt Missouri and Arkansas. Your pa's pap traded with me. I come in on it when Hobart and Dan was at it, tooth and nail. Hobart threatened to kill Dan and they had a big fight. Fists and knives. Dan cut Hobart pretty good and laid him up. Him and Clare got married whilst Hobart was in the infirmary. They had to push his bowels back in his belly and sew him up like a Christmas turkey."

"I never heard any of this."

"Well, Dan went and came to work for me and then we got the gold fever. Never saw hair ner hide of Hobart until that day he jumped our claim and you and me saw him and his bunch kill everybody in sight. But Hobart was carryin' a grudge, all right. It warn't no accident he come up to our camp."

"Why in hell didn't you say something to

me when we were up in that mine looking down at all the slaughter?"

"You was carryin' enough on your shoulders right then. I didn't see no sense in makin' things worse."

"It couldn't have been any worse."

"Yep, it could have been a sight worse, Johnny. If you'd have known who Hobart was, you'd have gone down there bare-handed and got yourself kilt. For no reason."

"But to kill my mother . . ."

"To Hobart that don't make no never-you-mind. He kilt his own mother. He was wrong from the first squall, that boy. Everybody in town knew it. Everybody was too scared of him to do anything about it. That bastard should have been put in a gunny sack with rocks and throwed in the river with the cats."

"I wonder if they knew," John said softly.

"Who knew?"

"The folks. I wonder if they knew it was Hobart who killed them."

Ben loosed a sighing breath that was almost like a whispered scream a man might hear in a nightmare. John looked over at Ben, wondering if he had any answer to such an unanswerable question.

"I reckon they knew. Your pa, leastwise."

"He recognized Hobart after such a long

time, you mean."

"I don't know if he even saw him, but your pa told me once, after he and Clare come up to Missouri and worked my land, that he figured Hobart wouldn't give up on Clare."

"What did Pa say?"

"He said somethin' like, 'Ollie ain't one to give up on what he wants real bad. He's like a snake you think you drove away and then it comes sneakin' back when you ain't lookin'.'"

"Pa said that?"

"He figured him and Ollie would meet up again some day. Said somethin' about it being Fate, like Fate was writ down in a man's book and warn't nothin' he could do about it."

John said nothing for several moments as the two rode side by side up the well-traveled but deserted road.

"I reckon, Ben, that Fate had me in its book, too."

"What do you mean, Johnny?"

"Well, if Fate is written down in a man's book, Ollie's name is in there, and mine, too."

"You could look at it that way, I reckon."

"That's the way I look at it, Ben."

Ben sucked that spent sigh back in, like it

was something he couldn't get rid of and he held it like a man holds his breath when he knows something bad is going to happen, but he just doesn't know exactly when.

8

The two riders were shadows, drifting through the Wyoming twilight like weary vagabonds on some forgotten desert with an unpronounceable Arabic name. The lights of Cheyenne glimmered in orange flames behind them like flickering oil lamps in Bedouin tents. They had ridden into the town and ridden right out, picking up the supplies they needed, separated, their hat brims pulled low, their movements furtive but deliberate.

Army Mandrake had not expected a posse to catch up to them so soon, but he wasn't taking any chances. Dick Tanner, haggard from the long, hard ride up from Denver, was suspicious of everyone. He kept a hand in front of his face the entire time he was in the store buying supplies.

"You look like a damned owlhoot," Mandrake had said when they met up at the edge of town, each with enough grub to last them until they reached Fort Laramie.

"Well, what the hell, Army, that's what I am. You, too."

"You don't have to look like one. 'Specially in town."

"Hell, that ain't no town. Stinks of cow-shit and stale whiskey."

"Did you get whiskey?"

"I got enough to carry us to the fort," Tanner said.

"You better."

"Fuck you, Army," Tanner said. "When my cousin gets there, I'm going to tell him what a stupid thing you did back in Denver."

"Hell, he probably knows already," Mandrake said.

He thought of the knife in its sheath, hanging from his belt. It still had blood on it, and he liked that. He had taken it out several times, whenever they stopped to rest their horses, just to look at the dried blood and remember slitting a man's throat, seeing his life drain out of him pretty as you please. Blood held a fascination for Mandrake. Ever since he had killed his first chicken, his first rabbit, he enjoyed watching the blood drain out of a creature, rendering it permanently lifeless.

He had killed his own father, stabbing him to death during an argument at home. His mother had seen it. She had screamed and Army had just stood over his father watching him bleed to death on the kitchen table. That was the first man he had killed, and after that, all killings of animals had paled by comparison. That was his kinship with Ollie, he knew. Ollie had a different reason for killing, though. Ollie killed to get even with someone. Mandrake had no such restrictions on his blood habit. He killed because he liked the power it gave him to see a man's lifeblood flow from his body. It made him a little crazy when it happened. Crazy and happy all at once. And he liked to use a knife because when the blood spurted onto his hand he knew that he was in command. Life was his to take. Death was his to give.

"What kind of whiskey did you get, Dick?" Mandrake asked.

"Old Taylor. Ollie's favorite. And mine."

"You boys got good taste."

"Let's change the subject, Army. I smelt so much whiskey back in town, my throat and belly's got a hankerin' for a swaller."

"We got to make tracks is all I know."

"Who we meetin' up with in Fort Laramie? Forget his name."

"Cresswell. George Cresswell. He's one of 'em."

"Yeah, and the other'n's somebody named Bosey, or somethin' like that."

"Bodie. Tucker Bodie."

"You know 'em, Army?"

"I know Tuck. Don't play cards with him and don't turn your back on him."

The twilight faded, taking with it the glow that had defined the snowcapped peaks of the Medicine Bows, plunging the earth into a darkness that removed all definition of rocks, plants, landmarks, the road itself. A chill crept over the land as the first stars brightened, winked, and glimmered like the lights of distant villages on a vast plain. Nighthawks that had scoured the dusk sky seemed to vanish all of a sudden, leaving behind only a hush that triggered the scratchy jabber of crickets, now seemingly safe from preying birds.

"What about Cresswell? Who's he?"

"Supposed to meet him at a saloon in town. Ollie said he'll tell us what to do."

"Steal rifles is what I heard."

"I think they done been stole, Dick, was what Ollie told me."

"Army rifles?"

"Yep."

"Military?"

"Uh-huh."

"I got a bad feelin' about that, Army."

"Why?"

"There's a fort there. We'll have soldiers down on us like chicken feathers stuck to hot tar."

"Don't you fret about that, Dick."

"How come?"

"Cresswell."

"Cresswell? I guess I don't get it. He got a bigger pecker than me or you?"

"You'll find out, I reckon."

"Damn it, Army. You're bein' mighty mysterious. I got to drag this all out of you like pullin' possums out of the sorghum jar. Who in hell is Cresswell?"

"Well, you're gonna find out, so might as well tell you."

"Go on then, damn it."

"He's Major Cresswell. And he's in charge of the armory at Fort Laramie."

Tanner let out a long whistle. It died in the evening air, in the silence.

They rode on as the moon rose, casting a pale light over the country. Eerie shapes appeared, changed form, then disappeared as if they were wandering through a desolate dreamscape where nothing was as it seemed and none of it made sense.

"Where are these rifles going to?" Tanner asked after a while.

71

"If I knew, Dick, I wouldn't tell you."

"You don't know?"

"Nope."

"Doesn't seem like a big money deal to me. But Ollie wouldn't be in it unless there was."

"You're smarter than you look, Dick."

"Hell, I don't give a damn. But army rifles ain't gold."

"Don't be too sure about that," Mandrake said.

"Now you're bein' mysterious again."

"Somewhere in all this, you can bet your ass there's gold, Dick. Or Ollie wouldn't be ridin' to meet us in Fort Laramie."

Tanner's horse dropped a few steps behind Mandrake's. He whipped his mount's shoulders with the rein tips and touched spurs to his flanks until the horse caught up.

"Well, that perks me up some," Tanner said. "Gold. But I sure as hell don't know who'd pay gold for some Spencer carbines."

"Me, neither," Mandrake said.

And so they rode on toward Fort Laramie, the mystery hovering between them, the speculation roiling in their minds like a floating stick caught in a whirlpool, submerging and emerging, going around and around and never getting anywhere.

The air turned chill and the moon painted

the land with soft pewter as shadows and brush danced in and out of moonlight, silent as the wraiths that floated in their puzzled minds.

9

Ben and John made camp that night on the prairie, far enough from the road that their fire could not be seen. And, as Ben remarked, there was so much open space, they could see or hear anyone coming for some distance.

"I got hard bones in my butt I never knew were there before," Ben said as he unsaddled Dynamite. "I'm plumb stove up, Johnny."

"Well, you'll work those kinks out of your rope when you finish gathering us some firewood."

"You ain't sore?" Ben wore a look of exasperation on his face, evident by the way his lips peeled back from his teeth and his forehead wrinkled up with four deep furrows.

"Some," John said. "Neither of us is used to the saddle, I reckon."

"Oh, I'm used to the saddle," Ben said. "It's Dynamite's blamed stiff legs I can't abide. I swear, it felt like I was getting hit with a pile driver every step that blamed horse took."

"Sleep on your belly tonight, Ben."

Ben stopped grumbling after John had a fire going. He sat on two folded-up horse blankets and kept shifting his weight from one buttock to the other as sparks rose skyward like golden fireflies and the skillet sizzled with bacon and the biscuit dough rose and browned, releasing heady aromas into the air.

They ate in silence. John never looked into the fire, but up at the stars or out onto the dark plain. The coffeepot burbled as the water boiled and Ben sniffed that scent, too, a contented smile on his face. He leaned close to the steam and caught the aroma in his nostrils. John listened to the horses chewing on the grain in their feedbags and watched a distant patch of winking stars.

He tried not to think about the dead woman, her husband, and her son, but he felt their presence as if their spirits were among the stars, sailing in a barque along the grand river of the Milky Way.

The fire began to burn down. Neither Ben nor John added any more fuel, so the burning wood would eventually die out and become embers.

"Ben, you said something back there at that wagon when I was looking at the — the dead woman."

"Yeah? I might have."

"You said I was looking at eternity."

"Yeah, I reckon. Kind of."

"What did you mean, exactly?"

"I dunno, Johnny. I reckon we feel most mortal when we see the body of someone who's been livin', breathin', talkin' and all the life and breath gone out of 'em."

"But it's more than that, isn't it? I mean, we are mortal. We're all going to die. Sooner or later."

"Yep. Way I figger it, we go from eternity to eternity. Life is just a little rest stop on the wayside."

"You mean . . . ?"

"Well, I didn't mean it so serious back there. But yeah, I been thinkin' on it for some time. Maybe more since Ollie and his bunch killed all of our friends and kinfolk right in front of our eyes. I figure we come from somewhere, maybe someplace eternal, and when we die, we just go back there."

"How? Why?"

Ben snatched a clump of sage, pulled it from the ground, shook off the dirt, and tossed it on the smoldering fire. A fragrant aroma rose with the smoke.

"I don't know how ner why, and nobody on this earth does, Johnny. It's nothin' to fret about, the way I see it. When I was a boy, down in Arkansas, my pa knowed an old Osage Injun. I used to go down by the creek and talk to this feller, name of Green Bow. He said his people believed that they come here from the Spirit World and when they die, they go back to that world."

"You believe that, Ben?"

"I don't know what I believe. I know when we went to the arbor church I kept listenin' to see if any of the preachers agreed with old Green Bow."

"And?"

"I reckon they didn't, leastwise in them same words."

John was silent for several moments. Ben kept adding sage to the fire. The heady scent was strong in their nostrils and the smoke was thick and gray.

"I've puzzled over it some, too," John said after a time. "Ever since . . . since, you know . . ."

"Yep, I know. I think a man puzzles over death all his life, one way or t'other."

"Doesn't do any good, does it, Ben? We never find out. Never learn the answers."

"Nope. Not until we come to that last door."

"Last door?"

"The one we come in, I reckon. The one that leads us back to eternity."

"Does that give you comfort, Ben?"

John stretched his legs and wriggled his toes inside his boots. He watched the smoke rise like a fakir's rope and then disappear in the blackness of the sky.

"Way I figger it, John, it don't make no difference what you believe. They's some who says when we're dead, we're plumb dead and there ain't no afterlife. If that's so, then we don't have no memory of this life and don't go nowhere. We just was and that was that. But if there is somethin' beyond that door, well, then the preachers was right all along and we'll know the answer. Either way, it don't matter much right here and now."

John drew a deep breath and let out a sigh.

"I'm sleepy as hell, Ben. You want to take the first watch?"

"Yeah. I'll walk around and maybe them bones in my butt will soften up some. You get some shut-eye and ponder all this talk."

John smiled.

"You know, Ben, for an old bird, you're pretty smart sometimes."

"Aw, Johnny. I was just talkin'. Nothin' I said you need to take to heart."

"I'm not so sure, Ben."

John laid out his bedroll, unhitched his gunbelt, and rolled it up, setting it within easy reach. He loosened the pistol in its holster and set the holster at an angle where he could pull the gun out fast if need be.

Ben stood up and flexed his legs, twisted his body at the waist, and rolled his shoulders up and down. He pulled his rifle from its scabbard and began to walk away from the camp. He started his circle within sight of John and the smoking fire. He stopped every so often to look and listen. In the distance, he heard a coyote yap and then there was only a deep silence.

The moon sailed ever higher in the sky, and small, thin clouds floated between it and the earth, glowing ghostly as they drifted among the distant stars.

He thought of John Savage and his questions. He saw that as a good sign. Maybe he wouldn't be so quick with that gun of his from now on. Maybe he would begin to take death as seriously as Ben did and give up trying to avenge the death of his parents.

But he knew that wasn't true. John might question death in a philosophical sense, but his hatred for Ollie Hobart was stronger than any words of discouragement he might hear. No, Johnny was bound and determined to rub out Ollie Hobart, sending him back to eternity or straight to hell.

10

Ollie and Rosa rode into the outskirts of Cheyenne shortly before noon. They were both weary, horses and clothes covered with a patina of reddish dust, both reeking with sweat. Rosa began patting her hair and combing it with her fingers, trying to draw back the dangling strands that strayed downward from beneath her hat.

"You've got some of the afternoon, Rosa, to clean up, buy yourself some duds, and sleep on a soft bed. We'll leave Cheyenne before nightfall."

"Where are we going now?" she asked.

"There's a hotel and saloon right up the street where I always stay. I'll get us a room and then meet up with you later."

"What are you going to do, Ollie?"

"Feller I want to see at the Frontier, right next to the hotel."

"Are you not going to rest? Surely, we will take a lunch together. Does the hotel have a dining room?"

"No, you'll have to eat by yourself. Yes, there's a dining room in the Excelsior. Just don't eat any of their pork."

"I do not like pork. *Puercos. Animales susios.*"

Ollie laughed and they turned up a small street, then up another, the first nearly deserted, the second lined with small shops. Indians sat in front of some of the stores, surrounded by woven blankets, beaded bracelets, necklaces, and clay pottery.

At the end of the street, a clapboard hotel with the name Excelsior painted on its high front loomed taller than the other buildings. Next door to it was the Frontier Saloon, with the name Roscoe Bender, prop., painted beneath it.

"Not the Brown Palace," Rosa remarked, fluffing her dusty black hair hanging down the back of her neck.

Ollie chuckled. "This ain't Denver, neither. Smell the cowshit, Rosa?"

She sniffed and laughed. "I smell it."

They pulled up in front of the hotel, dismounted, and looped their reins around the hitchrail out front.

Four moonfaced Indian children rushed out into the street from the shadows between the buildings, their hands outstretched and their faces dirty. The two girls wore shabby dresses made from burlap, while the boys had on torn trousers that appeared to have been sewn together from scraps of cloth. All were barefooted.

"*Dinero, dinero,*" they chorused. Both boys and girls flashed gap-toothed smiles.

"Give them some money, Ollie," Rosa said, smiling at the children.

"Goddamned beggars," Ollie said. "Get out of here, you kids. Shoo."

He stepped toward them in a menacing manner and the children scattered like quail, scurrying away from the big man.

Rosa frowned. "You could have given them each a penny," she said.

"I hate beggars, Rosa. 'Specially Injun ones."

"They are poor," she said.

"I got no use for poor Injuns ner beggars. They was old enough to work."

She said something in Spanish under her breath about his parentage. Ollie ignored her, as she knew he would. He did not know much Spanish, mostly the curse words, the blasphemies, and those words that got him what he wanted. She knew he was not a very nice man, and the remark about Indians caused a twinge in her heart.

She had Indian blood in her veins, Yaqui,

and she knew the low status Mexicans held in the United States. Still, she cared for Ollie in a way she would have found hard to explain to anyone. She was drawn to him because of the power he held, the power over life and death, and the animal way he pursued money. She could understand the latter trait because she bore it herself. But the savagery of the man drew her to him like a fluttering moth to a flame. Perhaps, she thought, it was the animal in herself that made him attractive. Ollie lived with death, and her people knew death firsthand. The Mexican soil was soaked in it, and in her village in Jalisco, a man with blood on his hands stood taller than any other.

"I'll give you some money now, Rosa," Ollie said. "And get you a room. Then I got to tend to the horses, give 'em some water and feed, and see the man who owns the Frontier. Fifty dollars be enough?"

"Yes," she said, her voice tight with a controlled rage. She felt like a whore at that moment. She had left her cantina with no money, no clothes, and he was treating her like the beggars he said that he hated. He had money on him, she knew, much more than the amount he stole from those pilgrims they had killed north of Fort Collins. Yes, he was a savage, and so was she. She had the sudden desire to see a priest and confess all her sins, but she knew that she would not. If she did, she would have to take up residence in the confessional for many hours.

Ollie reached in his pocket and withdrew some bills. He peeled off five sawbucks and handed them to her. Then he strode toward the hotel with Rosa in his wake.

After he checked Rosa in and asked if someone could rub down their horses and give them grain and water, he watched her walk back to the room with her key.

"I want the horses saddled and back at that hitchrail out front in two hours," he told the clerk. "Think you can manage that?"

"Yes, sir, we have a reliable stable boy who can take care of all that."

"How much?"

"Three dollars ought to do it."

He gave the clerk three dollars, knowing most of it would go in his pocket. The stable boy would be lucky to get fifty cents of that money.

He walked out of the hotel and next door to the Frontier Saloon. There were no boardwalks on that street, but swampers, store owners, urchins, maybe, kept the dirt swept down. He stomped his boots to shake off some of the dust and entered the saloon, pushing aside the bat-wings, then stepping to one side until his eyes adjusted to the dim light.

Dust motes danced in the shaft of sunlight pouring through the entryway. Ollie's eyes narrowed and his right hand fell within reach of his pistol.

You just never know, he thought as he scanned the bar, the tables, watching for any odd movement or change of expression on any of the faces. Hardly anyone noticed him except the barkeep, who, while he had seen his share of hard cases over the years, recognized Hobart the moment he stepped through the swinging doors. Ollie's gaze swept the room twice, then settled on Sam Rafer, who nodded to him from behind the bar.

Ollie strode over to the very end of the dogleg and stood next to the wall. From there he could see the front door and the back hallways that led to Roscoe's office and out to the back alley.

"Ollie," Rafer said, striding to the end of the bar.

"Sam. Roscoe here?"

"Yeah, he's smokin' cigars and countin' his money back in the office. He'll be out directly."

There were three men and an older woman at the other end of the bar. Two men flanked the woman, who looked as if she had opened the saloon early that morning. Her eyes were bleary; she had too much rouge on her cheeks and too much red lipstick on her lips. She wore a tattered hat that had seen better days and her facial wrinkles were covered with a whitish powder that almost matched her hair. The two men on either side of her were nearly as old, and both looked worn out. The rouge on their cheeks was painted there by hard rotgut liquor and the veins in their noses looked like baby-blue runners frozen in putty.

Basque and Mexican sheepherders sat at the tables drinking cheap tequila and beer, their voices liquid with rapid Spanish, their gesticulating hands carving arabesques in the air like fluttering birds attached to brawny, brown-skinned arms.

"You got a lot of road on you, Ollie," Rafer said, looking at Hobart and the dust on his forehead and shirt.

"I got a lot of road in my throat, too, Sam. Need to wash some of it down."

"I got some Old Taylor. You want some water with it?"

"Naw, just a shot of Old Taylor. I've tasted your water before."

Rafer laughed and took a bottle from the well. He snatched a shot glass from the back counter on his way over, set it in front of Hobart. He poured the glass full.

"Want me to leave the bottle, Ollie?"

"Nope. This'll do me."

"Two bits."

Ollie put a quarter on the counter. He watched Sam put the bottle back in the well, then drank half of his whiskey, sucking it into his mouth, wallowing it over his teeth before swallowing. Rafer returned and stood opposite Ollie.

"Seen any of my boys around, Sam?"

"Nary. That bad?"

"No, that's good."

"You got something cooking?"

"Nope. But I'm gatherin' firewood."

Sam laughed. Just then they heard a door open, then the clump of boots on hardwood. A moment later, Roscoe Bender, a cigar stuffed in his jowly face, entered the saloon from the hallway. He wore a Colt Bisley on his belt, up high, and the holster was snugged up next to a long, skinny knife with a hole drilled in the handle that was threaded with a thong. Ollie knew that Roscoe usually had that Arkansas toothpick dangling down his back, within easy reach if he got into a brawl. He was surprised to see it hanging from his belt in plain sight.

"Here comes Roscoe now," Sam said, and moved away toward the sodden patrons at the other end of the bar.

Bender came up next to Ollie, looked him over with jaded, rheumy eyes set back behind high cheekbones like those of some feral animal's. He puffed on his cigar and blue smoke formed a cloud just over his head.

"Ollie, long time."

"Yeah."

"I heard you run into some gold."

"Some bigmouth tell you that?"

"Birds fly back and forth, from north to south."

"Roscoe, I got a job for you. Pays in paper or gold."

"Either way. Spends about the same. Ain't none of your boys around to do it?"

"Not many of my boys left, and none of 'em here."

"What you got, Ollie?"

"You're going to need more than that puny Bisley on your belt."

Roscoe didn't glance down at his pistol. He blew a plume of smoke out of the side of his mouth.

"This is my bar gun," he said. "It's more of a persuader and does real good up close."

"Two men on my trail, Roscoe. An old guy and a young whippersnapper. I don't want them to get any farther than Cheyenne. You'll have to meet 'em on the trail from Denver."

"I got two men can do the job."

"You got to be one of 'em. It's right important."

Ollie swallowed the rest of his whiskey.

"You sound real serious, Ollie."

"I'm serious. The boy's a fair shot with a Colt. He's rubbed out some of my boys."

"What's your offer, Ollie?"

"A hundred now, and I'll give you another two hundred when you give me the pistol that young feller's carryin'. I want proof."

"Hell, I could just give you a piece of hardware and tell you I done it."

"This boy's got a special pistol. Ain't no other like it. I want it."

"Sure, Ollie. You're payin' more'n anybody around here for a killin'. Hell, for twenty bucks, I could get burials for four men."

Ollie dug into his pocket and peeled off five twenty-dollar bills. He slipped them to Roscoe below the counter. Bender put the money in his pocket.

"They might be real close behind me, Roscoe," Ollie said.

"You be around?"

"Goin' to Fort Laramie. Be here till about four. If you bring me the pistol before then, I'll pay you off."

"You want me to go check the trail right now?"

"Right now, Roscoe."

"All right, Ollie. Another drink?"

Ollie shook his head.

"And you ain't got time to jaw with me, Roscoe. Take the longest rifle you got is my advice."

"You ain't scared, are you, Ollie? And this ain't the law on your tail?"

"No, I'm not scared and there's no law on my tail. Just that damned kid and the old geezer. I want their lamps put out permanent."

"Sure, Ollie. Make like it's already done."

Ollie snorted.

"Just bring back that pistol and keep it in the safe for me, Roscoe."

Roscoe stubbed out his cigar in an ashtray as Ollie walked toward the bat-wing doors. He watched him go outside, then beckoned to Sam.

"I'll be goin' out, Sam. You seen Dooley and Kerrigan this mornin'?"

Sam shook his head. But he knew if Roscoe wanted to see those two, somebody was going to wind up dead.

91

Sam swallowed as Roscoe walked back toward his office. Then he broke out in a clammy sweat that oiled his palms and wet his armpits. His throat went dry and he wanted a drink in the worst way.

"Yep," he said to himself, "somebody's sure as hell goin' to die."

11

Ben and John turned their horses toward the spring, following the tracks and a sign pointing the way. They rode up a draw that branched off in two directions. Another sign pointed to the location of the spring, and again, there were plenty of tracks to show them the way. At the head of the canyon, someone had erected a stone cairn in the shape of a horseshoe. Inside the horseshoe, there was a small pond that rippled with flowing water.

"Horses are mighty thirsty," Ben said. "You been pushing it, Johnny. My canteen's plumb empty and my butt bones are kickin' up again."

"Fill your canteen, Ben, and quit belly-achin'." John's eyes were on the tracks and the horse manure scattered around the spring in small piles.

"See!" Ben said. "You're getting as testy as me."

"I'm not testy," John said. "I'm calculating how far behind Hobart we are. He and that Delgado woman were at this spring."

"Maybe. But how long ago?"

"I'll know in about two minutes," John said as he swung down from his horse.

He and Ben filled their canteens, then let the horses drink from the low end of the pond where it spilled into a trickling stream that coursed a few yards, then went underground.

John walked around, examining each pile of horse manure. He matched tracks with offal and then went down on one knee. As Ben watched, John picked up a brown nugget from the top of the pile, cracked it in half, and smelled it. Then he touched the insides. He dug lower in the pile and picked up another, one of the first apples to fall. He did the same thing with that one, then stood up.

"Not good enough to eat?" Ben asked.

"Don't get smart, Ben. You can tell how old a chunk of horseshit is just by feeling how wet it is, how stale it smells."

"Where'd you learn that?"

"From my pa, only we were tracking deer or elk when he showed me what to do."

"And what does that horseshit tell you, Johnny?"

"If that's a smirk on your face, I might not answer you, Ben."

Ben made a show of straightening his face, wiping the faint smile from his lips and dragging his chin down until he bore a reasonably sober and serious expression on his visage.

"Hell, you can tell from the tracks how long it's been since they come here," Ben said. "I know you can do that."

"I can. But doing this backs up what I already know. And gives me a better line on how much time has passed since Ollie was here."

Ben took off his hat and scratched his head.

"I say maybe three hours, just lookin' at the tracks. Not much crumbled dirt in 'em. Mud's dried some. Three hours. Four at the most."

"You're sure, huh, Ben?"

"Reasonably sure."

John raked a pile of horse apples with his foot, spread them out. There was no steam, the insides were nearly dry. He looked up at the sky, shaded his eyes, raked a glance across the sun's position, avoiding a look into its fiery, blinding heart.

"I figure closer to six hours, maybe seven. Near a day's ride to catch up with them."

"How could they be that far ahead of us?" Ben asked.

"I didn't see them make a night camp. They've been riding all night."

"In an all-fired hurry, ain't he?" Ben asked.

"I was hoping to catch him in Cheyenne and be done with all this," John said.

Ben walked around, flexing his legs. John heard his knees crack and saw Ben wince. He drank from his canteen, then refilled it. He didn't know how far they were from Cheyenne, but maybe, he thought, since Ollie and Rosa had ridden all night without any sleep, they might hole up in Cheyenne for a day or so.

"You really think killing Ollie will end it for you, Johnny?" Ben asked, turning to face Savage, who was squatted down, refilling his canteen from the spring again.

"Yeah, I do. Ollie's the one I want."

John stood up, corked the wooden canteen, slung it over his saddle horn.

"Will that finish it for you, Johnny? Really?"

"I expect so. Why? You worried about something?"

"Ollie ain't the only one left out of that killing bunch."

"I know. If I run across the others, I

expect I'll call 'em out. Mandrake's one. Who's the other?"

"Dick Tanner."

"Yeah. I'm not going to waste time hunting those two. Ollie was the one who called the shots. When he's down, I'll ride on through the rest of my life."

"That won't end it," Ben said, his tone solemn.

John shot him a sharp look.

"So you say. What do you know?" John asked.

"Them other two. They'll be the same as you. They'll come after you. They'll want blood for blood."

"Let 'em come."

"And if you put them down? What then?"

"That should take care of it, I reckon," John said.

"You think so, Johnny? Hell, you cut yourself a long trail here. Be somebody after Mandrake and another after Tanner. And then another and another. Ain't no end to it."

John snorted.

"You know something, Ben? You just think too damned much."

"And you don't think enough. Give it up now, John. Let Hobart go. He'll meet his own end someday. It don't have to be you who finishes him off."

John felt the anger rise in him, as if from some well deep in his bowels licked by flames, the liquid turning to steam. His eyes narrowed and he licked his lips as if to quench the heat beginning to pour from him. He glared at Ben, sucked in a deep breath, closed his eyes for a moment, then opened them again to hot, black slits.

"Ben, you've been riding me and riding me about all this and I'm plumb fed up with your worrywart mouth and your simple platitudes. You don't like doing what you're doing, you can ride off right now, or wait until we get to Cheyenne. Either way suits me. I just want to get shut of you trying to talk me out of hunting down that bastard Hobart and sending him straight to hell with a forty-five slug. I've been tolerant of you, but I'm running out of patience and kindliness toward you."

Ben reacted as if John had come up to him and slapped him backhanded across the face. He froze for a moment and his face blanched. He balled up his fists, then relaxed his fingers, balled them up again, and flexed them back to normal.

"Johnny, you hadn't ought to have said what you did to me. But you said it and I'm just going to ask you one question before I ride on."

"One question," John said tightly.

Ben's eyes blazed with the coals of anger seething inside him.

"You got a conscience, Johnny?"

"What the hell kind of question is that?"

"You heard me. You got a conscience? You have a still, small voice inside you that whispers to you when somethin' ain't right and you got to think about doin' something bad before you do it?"

"I have a conscience, Ben. Yes."

"I reckon not."

"Who are you to judge whether I have a conscience or not?"

"Well, that's all I've been to you this whole time. I'm your conscience, Johnny, because you ain't got one. Now, you want to kick me in the ass and boot me out of your life. Hell, I'm the only conscience you got, son, and if I go, ain't nobody ner nothin' to tell you what's right and what's wrong."

There was a long silence between them, a thoughtful silence before either man spoke again.

Ben was the first to break.

"All right, Johnny Savage. I've said my piece, and you want it like this, I'll be on my way."

"Now just a damned minute, Ben."

Ben hesitated in mid-stride toward his horse.

Dynamite switched his tail and cocked his ears into rigid cones, staring walleyed at the two men. Gent, standing hipshot, lowered his left hind leg and shook his head, his mane rippling against his neck like the fringes on a Kiowa dancer's buckskin skirt.

"Yeah?" Ben said after several moments had passed.

"I got a conscience."

Ben waited for more, then shrugged.

"It talkin' to you now, Johnny?"

"Some, I reckon."

"And what's it sayin'?"

John sighed. He looked down at the ground, shook his head as if he was struggling with some inner demons. He raised his head and looked straight at Ben, eyes wide open.

"We've been friends a long time, Ben. You probably saved my life up in that cave. I was ready to go down and take on that whole outlaw bunch bare-handed."

"People forget such things all the time, Johnny."

"Well, I haven't forgotten. You've stuck with me and I know, in my heart, that most of what you say is well meant and probably good advice."

"Yeah?"

"Yeah, Ben. It's probably all good advice. For somebody else."

"It's meant for you, Johnny," Ben said quietly.

"I know. I know. It's just that I got this big hole inside me and it's got teeth and it gnaws at me. It wants me to take full measure of the wrong that man Hobart did to me and my family, and all the others who died up on that placer creek. Damn it, I have to go after Hobart. I want him to look into my eyes and see the pain I've been carrying ever since you and I buried all those good people. I want . . ."

"I know what you want, Johnny. I'm mad, too. I want revenge same as you. But remember what I told you."

"I remember. You said if I want revenge, I better dig two graves."

"That's right."

"If I don't make Hobart pay for what he did, who does?"

Ben walked over to John and put a hand on his shoulder. He looked John in the eyes with a kindly expression of his own.

"Maybe some things are best left to Fate or Judgment Day. Hell, I don't know. 'Vengeance is mine, sayeth the Lord.' That's in the Bible. Maybe you got to leave Hobart

101

to the Lord, if you believe in that sort of thing."

"Do you?"

"Most of the time," Ben said.

"Well, I've been thinking about that, too, Ben."

"What? Vengeance?"

"That, and other things. Like maybe if there is a God."

"And?"

"You never see him. Or hear him. And the Indians say he's the Great Spirit. That fits better in my mind than most of what the fire-and-brimstone preachers say. So, if he's a spirit, he can't do anything on his own. I mean he can make grass grow and rivers run, but he can't come down from Heaven and smite somebody with the jawbone of an ass or anything else."

"You making some kind of augur here, Johnny?"

"Maybe the Great Spirit uses people to carry out his wishes." John waited a few seconds. "You think maybe that's the way it is, Ben?"

"I don't know. Maybe."

"And maybe that conscience you talk about is Him telling us when something is right or wrong. But He still lets us choose, doesn't He?"

"I reckon."

John smiled.

"See? I've been working it all out in my own mind. Surely God doesn't want Hobart to get away with murdering so many people. Hell, he's killed three right here on the road to Cheyenne. God didn't stop him."

"Nope, he sure didn't, did he?"

"So let me go my own way. I made a vow over my pa's and ma's graves that I'd avenge their deaths. And Pa left me that pistol. It's the only thing of his I have. I think he and God, maybe, want me to use it. I took that as a sign. From the Great Spirit, maybe."

Ben took his hand from John's shoulder and reared back for another critical look at him. Then, he smiled.

"You know, Johnny," Ben said, "sometimes you make a lot of sense."

"You understand what I mean. Why I have to stay on this trail."

"It's maybe a danger trail, Johnny."

"And I'll ride it out."

"You want me to go with you?"

"Sure, Ben. I'm sorry I let my temper loose on you a while ago."

"That's all right. Let's ride it then, Johnny, that danger trail."

Ben went to his horse and climbed up into the saddle. John stepped into his saddle and moved Gent close to Ben.

"One more thing, Ben, about those two graves."

"Yeah?"

"I dug mine a long time ago, when I put my folks in the ground. So don't you worry none, hear?"

Ben shivered in the warm sun as Gent stepped out and headed back down to the road. John sat straight and tall in the saddle, like a man who feared nothing nor anyone. Ben loved John in that moment, and he respected him, too, for speaking his own mind and working things out for himself.

Maybe, God willing, that other grave would stay empty a good long time.

12

Two crows strutted along the corral fence, stopping every so often to peck at a kernel of cracked corn or a grain of dusty wheat. They looked like miniature preachers in black sacerdotal garb, the sun glinting on the sheen of their feathers, flashing black and green and blue. A horse in the corral watched them with wide-eyed suspicion as he stood at the feed trough just inside the shaggy cedar poles of the fence. Another horse, its neck arched, head down, slaked its thirst in the water trough, nibbling with rubbery lips, nostrils blowing little waves in the water as if to cool it all down as he drank in the heat of the seething yellow sun.

"Somebody's comin', Mitch," Roy Kerrigan said as he sat in a chair under the shade of the ramshackle porch.

Mitchell Dooley, on the top step, his lanky frame sprawled there with legs outstretched, looked up from the stick he was whittling on and squinted into the glare.

"Yeah, it looks like Bender."

"Bender? The damned mole who never sees the light of day?"

"It's Bender, all right. Seldom seen in sunlight."

Roy Kerrigan laughed and swatted at a bluebottle fly that buzzed around his face, attracted by the dried remnants of eggs and biscuits clinging to his chin. He was a redheaded string bean of a man, with blue eyes so pale they looked as if they were coated with whitewash. With his hat pushed to the back of his head, the scars on his face stood out in stark relief, blanched serpentine scrawls on weathered, suntanned skin.

"He must have something pretty big in his craw," Dooley said, drawing one leg up and putting a boot on the bottom step. He set the stick down on the edge of the porch and closed the blade of his barlow pocketknife. The bluebottle sizzled around his face and he waved it off with a tanned, leathery hand.

The two men waited for Bender to ride in close enough for positive identification. Dooley turned his head to look at Kerrigan and nodded.

"Yep, it's Roscoe hisself," Roy said. "In full daylight. If that don't beat all."

Mitch chuckled. They had never seen Bender except at night and seldom away from the Frontier. They often joked about Bender being a mole who stayed underground all of his life.

"Glad I found you boys to home," Roscoe said as he rode up.

"Light down, Roscoe," Mitch said. "Get out of the sun before you shrivel up and melt down like a damned candle."

"Don't have time, Mitch, and neither do you two. Roy, you and Mitch want to make a little quick money?"

"How much money?" Dooley asked before Kerrigan could answer.

"A double sawbuck in it for each of you," Bender said.

"Who we got to kill?" Kerrigan said, a flicker of a smile on his lips.

The two crows took flight when one of the horses rushed the fence to scare them off. Their caws filled the air as they flapped away like two scraps of black crepe caught up in a whirling dust-devil spout.

"A couple of cockleburs under Hobart's saddle."

"Ollie in town?" Dooley asked.

"He's leavin', and he doesn't want to look over his shoulder. These jaspers will be ridin' in from Denver."

"When?" Kerrigan asked.

"Sometime today or by mornin', I reckon. Ollie didn't really know. He wants me to go with you two."

"We get to keep any money they got on 'em?" Kerrigan asked. "Rifles, saddles, pistols, horses?"

"Yep. One's an old coot, the other a young pecker. Ollie wants his pistol. I got to take that, is all."

Dooley slid down the steps, stood up on the ground.

"Just the young feller's pistol?"

"That's right, Mitch."

"How come?"

"Proof we kilt 'em both, I reckon." Bender brushed a fly away from his face. The fly shone blue and green, like a tiny jewel, in the sun. His horse shook its head as the fly dove past its eyes with an angry buzz of its wings.

Kerrigan rose from his chair and stepped to the edge of the porch.

"Kinda peculiar way of showin' proof, ain't it, Roscoe?"

"I don't know," Bender said.

Kerrigan pulled a ready-made from his shirt pocket, fished out a box of matches, struck one, and lit the cigarette.

"Why not both pistols? How's Ollie to

know we kilt both of 'em?"

"I guess he figures if we get the kid's pistol, we'd have to kill the old man, too."

"That's a lot of shit," Kerrigan said.

"Look, if you don't want the job, say so," Bender said. "We ain't got a whole lot of time here. I got grub in my saddlebags, a bottle of whiskey for when the job's finished, and money to pay you boys. Hell, I don't know how long we're going to have to wait. These two jaspers could be ridin' into town right this minute."

"Let's do it, Roy," Dooley said. "Hell, we're turnin' to rust a-settin' here on the porch."

"I'm game," Kerrigan said. "It just sounds like a funny deal to me."

"You got the money on you, Roscoe?" Dooley said.

"I got it on me and I'll pay you when those two are laid out on the ground."

"Give us fifteen minutes or so to saddle up," Dooley said.

Twenty minutes later, the three men rode off across the railroad tracks and took to the Denver road. Kerrigan and Dooley were reading tracks, mostly carts and wagons, one or two single horse prints, some going south, a few north into town.

"Don't look like they come this way yet," Kerrigan said after an hour's ride.

"Let's find a good place to wait in ambush," Dooley said. "Want to flank the road?"

"If we can find a good spot."

"Got to be close enough to see them in the dark," Bender said. "Might have to wait that long."

"I don't see too good in the dark," Dooley said.

"You don't see too good in the daytime, Mitch," Kerrigan cracked.

"I see enough of you to make me plumb sick to my stomach, Roy."

Bender scanned both sides of the road. There was plenty of cover, most of it some distance from the road. He ignored the banter between Kerrigan and Dooley. His nerves were stretched taut as skin on a drumhead.

"Moon'll be up tonight," Kerrigan said, pointing to some rocky spires and jumbled rocks standing on broken ground some thirty yards from the road. "That looks to be a likely place. What do you think, Mitch?"

"Might be good if all three of us can take cover there. Have to hobble the horses some ways away, though."

Bender breathed a sigh of relief.

"You boys have done this more'n once," he said.

"You're lookin' at the Drygulch Twins, Roscoe," Dooley said.

"The Bushwhacker Boys," piped up Kerrigan.

Bender didn't laugh as they rode toward the rock outcroppings, the wind-sculpted spires.

"Not a bit of shade," Kerrigan said as they rode up.

"That's what your damned hat's for, Roy," Dooley said.

"Roscoe, you should have brought some shade with you, a tarp or somethin'," Kerrigan said.

Bender looked up at the sky. The sun was at its zenith, straight overhead. High noon.

"Maybe we won't have to wait all that long, Roy."

"Well, you cast enough shadow, Roscoe. I'll just hunker up under your fat old butt."

Dooley laughed.

Kerrigan led the horses some distance away, until he could no longer see the hiding place. He hobbled each of them and walked back, carrying his rifle and an extra bandanna.

They sweated and waited for several hours, watching the road. Few people

111

passed. Those who did never noticed them, and none from the south fit the description Ollie had given Roscoe.

The sun fell away in the sky and finally began to paint shadows that pointed east. The shadows grew long and the last of the heat shimmers faded away. The western sky was ablaze with a fiery sunset that hung there beyond the Medicine Bows like some brilliant painting fashioned from iron and smoke.

"Where in hell are them two?" Kerrigan said as he lit another cigarette. "All the shade's on the other side of these damned rocks."

"You'll be freezin' your balls off, Roy, in another half hour," Dooley said.

Kerrigan wiped the sweat off his rifle with one of his bandannas. He blew smoke into the still, dry air.

Bender chewed on a dry biscuit and swallowed water from his canteen.

Dooley kept putting his ear to the ground, listening for hoofbeats.

The silence and the dark overcame the three men and still they waited. It was cool and the stars winked and blinked from far out in space. The moon rose, ever so slowly, and the men flexed their toes inside their boots to get their blood working.

They kept waiting. And watching. And listening.

Mitch and Roy were ready to kill and have that drink of whiskey that Roscoe had promised them.

13

Ben held on to his saddle horn with both hands. He swayed in the saddle, half asleep, nodding, then jerking back awake as Dynamite plodded on under a canopy of stars and a bright sailing moon.

"Ben, you're going to fall if you don't stay awake," John said.

"Why in hell can't we stop and get some damned sleep, Johnny?"

"We can't stop because Hobart didn't stop."

"There's no need for this."

"I'm not going to be bested by that bastard, Ben, so stay awake."

"I'm tryin', John. How come you're not sleepy?"

"I am sleepy, but here, bite on one of these."

John reached into his pocket. Ben heard some clicking sounds. A moment later, John handed him something.

"What is it?" Ben asked.

"A coffee bean. I got some out of my saddlebag about two hours ago. I didn't know if it would work or not, but I've eaten three or four and I don't feel as sleepy. I've got more if that one doesn't work."

Ben put the bean in his mouth, worried it around. He bit down on it. The bean was hard as a rock. John heard the sound of Ben's teeth trying to crack the bean.

"It'll take a while, Ben. Just keep it wet and keep crunching."

"Are you foolin' me, John?"

"Try it, Ben."

"Where'd you learn about this little trick, Johnny?"

"Ma told me not to drink coffee at night. She said it would keep me awake. I tried it once, drinking coffee after supper. And she was right. I couldn't get to sleep. So I thought if we couldn't boil coffee from horseback, maybe there was something in those beans that sparked a man's blood or brain and would keep me awake."

"If that don't beat all," Ben said and crunched down on the bean again.

After a while, Ben asked for another bean. John gave him two.

"It works, I think," Ben said. "Or maybe just tryin' to soften that bean enough to chew it is what's keepin' me awake."

John said nothing, but smiled in the darkness. He was thinking about his mother and the smell of coffee in the morning when he was a small boy. She would have the pot boiling before either he or his father was awake and the aroma was pleasant. It wafted through the house and both father and son knew that breakfast would be on the table before sunup.

There would be toasted bread and marmalade, fresh buttermilk chilled in the springhouse, and sometimes bacon and griddle cakes and sorghum, churned butter and soft-boiled eggs, prunes or persimmons, ripe plums or blueberries, all laid out on their table like a king's feast.

Unbidden tears stung John's eyes as he thought about his mother and his father. All he had now were memories and each recollection of bygone days pulled him deeper into a well of sadness, a consciousness of how much he had lost. Hobart had taken his mother and father away from him and there was no getting them back. There were just these empty holes in his life, an empty house, an empty room. An empty heart.

"That helps, for sure," Ben said.

"Huh? What helps?" John pulled himself out of his reverie with a jolt, oddly disoriented. He had forgotten all about Ben and where they were, where they were going.

"Them coffee beans. Almost like drinkin' white lightnin'."

"Good. I'd hate like hell if you fell out of the saddle and broke your bones."

Ben chuckled.

"The way I was, wouldn't have broke nothin', Johnny. I was limp as a wet bar rag."

"Stay with me, Ben. It's only a while until daybreak."

"Yeah, I must have dozed pretty deep. I was dreamin', dreamin' of my brother, Leland. Poor Lee."

Suddenly, John felt very selfish. He had hardly thought of Leland, or his own sister, Alice, but only of his mother and father, murdered on that same day when Hobart and his savage minions attacked their mining camp. And he had hardly thought of his uncle Don. Donald French was his mother's brother and had always been kind of like a big brother to him.

"We . . . we lost some good people that day, Ben," John said, realizing how awkward that sounded as soon as he had said it. "Damned good people."

"Lee had his best years ahead of him. And little Alice, your kid sister. I can't think of her without chokin' up and tears comin' to

117

my eyes."

"We better not talk about this, Ben, or we'll never get to Cheyenne. We'll have to stop and pray for all those folks we lost, all those now dead and gone."

"Yeah, Johnny, I know. Hard to forget, though."

"We won't ever forget, Ben. Ever."

They were silent for a time, the horses rolling along in an easy walking gait under a star-filled sky that seemed even more immense and mysterious now that their thoughts had turned to their dead kin. Way off in the distance, a pack of coyotes started yipping and trilling, their chromatic cries rising and falling like some surreal chorus in an outdoor cathedral, their eerie calls sounding like lost souls in both men's tortured hearts. The belling continued for several moments and then faded away, leaving only the overtones humming in their minds along that desolate road. Shadows loomed up and vanished, pewter landscapes appeared, so silent and bleak it felt as if the earth had swallowed up all hope, all goodness, all clear light, leaving only sheets of hammered iron lying in the bare stretches, dead plants and ghostly shapes in between, like small islands on a vast, empty sea.

John knew that the closer they got to

dawn, the more dangerous their journey would be. Not only were he and Ben tired, but the light would become trickier just before the sun came up, when the stars began to fade and the moon was setting. He did not know how far they were from Cheyenne, but he knew the horses were eating up the miles at a steady pace.

Ahead, he thought, Hobart and Rosa Delgado could be waiting in ambush, ready to pick them off with rifles. Or Hobart could have met up with cronies in Cheyenne and returned to bushwhack them before they even got to the settlement. These were worries he kept to himself because he didn't want to alarm Ben. But his senses were prickling as the night began to age and he could feel changes in the temperature.

"I wonder if we might not want to get off this road until we get to Cheyenne," Ben said an hour later.

"Have you been reading my thoughts?" John asked.

"You got that same feeling, Johnny?"

"What feeling?"

"About bein' the onliest ones on this road and it bein' dark as pitch. Hobart could be waiting in the brush for us, him and that Mexican gal."

"It occurred to me. The closer we get to

dawn, the harder it's going to be to see ahead of us."

"Yeah, and might not see nothin' until it's too late," Ben said.

"Wouldn't hurt to ride over some rough country until sunup. Keep us awake."

"Yeah. Might just save our lives, too," Ben said.

The two men turned their horses to the east and got off the road.

"Just let the horses pick their way through this brush," Ben said. "Take it slow."

"Good idea," John said.

After a time, the sky in the east began to pale. John rubbed his eyes as his vision shifted. Clumps of grass and brush changed shape, lost all definition. He could no longer see the ribbon of road off to the west and the mountains seemed to move toward them, then retreat, each time he looked in that direction.

Light spilled over the eastern horizon like cream rising in a bowl. Suddenly rocks and brush began to take shape and cast shadows. The mountains seemed to be etched out of darkness, and John could see the folds and contours of the foothills, the faint bristle of trees on the slopes. The dawn light moved slowly across the land, bringing nearby objects into sharp relief as if created on the spot by a master sculptor. He stretched in the saddle, yawned, and in his mind, he could hear a rooster crow, as if he had been transported back home to the family farm.

"Gettin' light," Ben said, as if he had just now noticed it.

"No," John cracked. "I thought it was getting darker."

"Aw, Johnny. I guess I deserved that. But after all that dark, mornin's like a miracle to me."

He, too, stretched in the saddle as if just awakening in his bed and John laughed at the mirror image of himself.

"Keep a sharp eye out, Ben."

"Can't make out much now."

"Just watch for anything out of place along that road yonder."

"Like what?" Ben asked.

"Hell, I don't know. Anything. Hobart. The Mexican woman. Somebody standing on a rock with spyglasses up to his eyes."

"A mite testy ain't ye, Johnny? Like your nerves was rubbed raw with sandpaper."

"I'm tired, Ben. Bone tired."

"Hell, who ain't? Horses, too. Look at 'em, all bleary-eyed and droopy. I was just wonderin' what you expect me to see, that's all."

"I'm not expecting you to see a damned thing, Ben. Just keep your eyes peeled, that's all. I don't trust Hobart."

"Me, neither," Ben said and shot John a sullen glance. He made a show of looking ahead, over toward the road. He stood up in the stirrups, then sank back down in the saddle.

John wanted to swat him.

White streamers of clouds in the northern sky turned salmon, the air chilled a few degrees as the sun sucked up the cold from the ground, the scent of sagebrush and buffalo grass wafted to their nostrils. John scanned the horizon ahead, edged his horse toward the road for a better look at the way ahead.

There were no wagons, no riders, no carts at that hour. Ben followed him and they rode parallel to the road.

"Clean as a billiard ball," Ben said after a time.

"What?"

"That road's empty as a pauper's pocket."

"Yeah. He won't be on the road, Ben."

"Oh, where will he be? A-floatin' like a hawk in that blue sky? Crawlin' through the brush like a lizard?"

"Eat another coffee bean, Ben. You're plumb delirious from lack of sleep."

"Hell, I'm just conversin', Johnny, making light of the situation."

John opened his mouth to say something clever or cruel, but something caught his eye and he held up a hand, reined in Gent, slowing the horse down.

"Hold up, Ben."

"Huh?"

John pulled his horse to a halt. He stared across the road, fixed on a rocky outcropping some five hundred yards or so distant.

"I thought I saw something," John said.

"On the road?"

"No, a hundred yards or so off to the left. See those spires yonder? That jumble of something that looks like rocks? Off there in the flat, with nothing much else around it?"

Ben swept the land with his gaze, his head turning slightly. Then he stopped.

"I see something. Rocks, I reckon. Can't make out much else. What'd you see, Johnny?"

"I don't know. Might have been nothing." John's voice was very soft, almost a whisper.

He closed his eyes, squeezed them tight with his muscles, then opened them again.

He stared at the rocks, the thin reddish spires jutting up, making a visible silhouette.

"There," John said. "See it?"

"What?"

"A glint. Like something silver or gold. A flash, just to the left of that rocky spire sticking up like a petrified stick."

They sat there, both staring at the same place.

Several seconds passed as the sun rose higher in the sky. The land glowed with its light and the rocks stood out in stark relief. A light breeze blew warm against their cheeks.

Then a flash of light struck their eyes, and another, as if the sun's rays were glancing off a pair of mirrors.

"Shit, oh shit," Ben murmured. "Right there in them rocks. Somebody's a-settin' there, just waitin' for somebody to pass by. Ooooohhhweee. Just a-settin' there pretty as you please."

"Wish I had a pair of binoculars," John said.

"Hell, you don't need 'em. I can see pretty good. There's at least two jaspers hidin' behind them rocks, and that sparkle was right off a couple of rifle barrels."

"Hobart?" John breathed.

"Hobart, I don't know. But whoever's there ain't huntin' jackrabbits. We better light out, John, fast as we can git."

"No, they've likely seen us."

"We got a good head start. We ride east

and put a hell of a lot of distance between us."

"No. Hobart wants a showdown, we'll give him one."

"Are you plumb crazy, John? We're out in the open. They got them rocks for cover."

John thought about it. He surveyed the terrain, assessed their chances. He didn't know how many men they were facing, but at least two, maybe three or four. His empty stomach felt queasy.

He had a decision to make and their lives hung in the balance.

Neither man spoke for several minutes.

Quick spurts of dazzling lights shot from the rocks. Not quartz, not mica, not embedded gold. Rifles.

"John?"

"I've made up my mind, Ben. We can do it."

"Do what?"

John didn't answer right away. He was still mulling over the skeleton of a plan. Seconds ticked by as he worked over the last details, went over every action in his mind.

The stillness was as loud as thunder in his ears. His mouth was as dry as desert dust.

He waited as his nerves stretched tighter and tighter like a thin wire holding a metal basket filling up with anvils, the basket getting heavier and heavier, the wire tautening until it was as thin as a strand of the finest hair.

14

John turned his head and looked at the eastern horizon. Then he held up a hand in front of his eyes, closed off all but three fingers. He held the three fingers up to block off a space just above the horizon.

"What're you doin', John?" Ben asked.

"A little trick Pa showed me when we were hunting," John said.

"Holding up three fingers?"

"We did it mostly at the end of the day, just before sunset."

"I don't want to sound stupid," Ben said, "but what the hell for?"

"Each finger is roughly fifteen minutes. If you hold your hand up just under the spot where the sun is, you can tell how long it'll be before sunset."

"Does it really work?"

"Every time," John said.

"So this is morning."

"I want to see how long it will take the

sun to rise above the horizon so that it shines directly into the eyes of whoever is laying for us behind those rocks."

The sun was just barely above the horizon. It glowed with an orange flame, shimmered with a blinding brilliance.

"And how long do you figure?" Ben asked.

"A little over fifteen minutes should be about right."

"You don't aim to ride straight into them guns?"

"I sure do," John said.

"You're plumb crazy. We ought to just hightail it and ride east in a big old loop."

A quail piped a solitary lyric somewhere to the north of them. In the thin, still air, the sound carried a long way. Nothing stirred nearby and John kept staring at the rocks. Every so often, he saw a glimmer of light.

"They'd be on us like hair on a bear, Ben. We'd run our horses to death trying to stay ahead of them. No, I've got a plan that might work. A little risky, but the odds are in our favor."

"You a gambler now?" Ben's voice was thick with sarcasm.

"We've got the sun at our backs. If we start riding toward them real slow, they'll sit tight until we're within a certain range."

"Yeah, that's what I'm afraid of. We get within a hunnert yards and they'll pick us off like turtles on a swamp log."

"We're going to ride toward those rocks single file, Ben. Me in the lead. We're both going to hunker down so we don't give them a target until we get close to a hundred yards from them. Then, when I say the word, we're going to put the spurs to these horses and ride like hell, pistols cocked. If I zig, you zig. If I zag, you zag."

"Suicide, that's sure as hell what it is, Johnny."

"I'm counting on those bushwhackers to get all rattled when we charge in on them. By the time we get within pistol range, they'll have empty rifles and wet pants."

Ben slid his hat back and scratched his forehead.

"That's the craziest idea I ever heard," Ben said.

"Maybe, but it's the only idea I have."

"It might work."

"They won't expect us to ride straight at them."

"No, 'cause they're probably not loco."

"That sun's going to blind them for fair."

"If we time it right, it might play hob with their eyes, all right."

"We can cover a hundred yards at a gallop

faster than they can figure out what we're doing, I think."

"Still, we're out in the open. They got rocks to pertect 'em."

"My guess is they'll step out and try to pick us off with their pistols. Once we're close enough, I'll yell and you break off from behind me and start spitting lead at them. First bullet they hear coming, they'll dive for the dirt."

"You think."

"Well, I have to figure they're not just going to stand there with empty rifles or try to stuff cartridges in the magazines."

"You give this a heap of thought, did you, Johnny?"

John looked at the sun again, a quick glance so he wouldn't burn his eyes. More of the blazing disk had slid up over the horizon, and more was coming.

"Let's start now," he said to Ben. "You fall in right behind me and hunker down low. Stay as close as you can and just watch Gent's rump."

"Not an appetizin' sight, Johnny."

"It'll keep you alive, Ben."

"So you say." Ben spat and reined Dynamite in behind Savage.

John took one more measurement with his fingers, then touched the blunt spurs to

Gent's flanks. They started moving toward the rock pile. Now, Savage thought, he would have to tick off seconds in his mind. Keep track of time and hope he was right. The timing was everything, and still, he knew he was taking a big chance. He didn't know how many men he was facing, but he figured at least two. And it could be Hobart and that Delgado woman.

He kept his eyes on the rock spires, kept Gent on a straight line. His stomach knotted up as the distance shrank. He still couldn't make out how many rifles he was facing, but he was looking for movement. Whoever was behind those rocks must be wondering what he was doing riding straight at them. Maybe they were counting their chickens before they were hatched, thinking he was just curious.

He sat straight in the saddle. When he looked at Ben out of the corner of his eye, not moving his head very much, he saw that Ben was hugging his horse's neck, flattened out on the saddle like a griddle cake.

He had to figure time and distance. He measured the distance with his eyes, hoping he was right. He would soon know. They were still at a walk and the rocks looked closer. Were closer. He figured they were less than four hundred yards from the rifles by then. And none of the bushwhackers had moved from their hiding place.

He expected one of them might lie flat next to the rocky outcropping to steady himself for the first shot. So far he was only seeing those blinding glints of sunlight bouncing off rifle barrels.

Three hundred yards, John figured, and his hands were sweating. His pistol was still in his holster, but he was ready to draw and cock whenever it was time.

Two hundred yards and closing, he thought. Perspiration dripped down from his armpits, soaking through the back of his shirt. He wiped his forehead and hunkered down slightly, peering past Gent's neck straight at the outcropping.

He heard Ben clear his throat and then spit again.

It was quiet except for the soft thud of the horses' hooves on dry ground, or the crunch of a twig, the rustle of sage. Even the quail were silent, and there wasn't a bird or a hawk in the sky.

The mountain shadows rose higher and higher and John could measure the sun's height just by looking beyond the rocks.

When he thought he was close to a hundred yards from the site of the ambush, John drew his pistol.

"When I start running, Ben, you stay right with me."

"We're gettin' mighty close, I figger."

"You might hear one of them shoot."

"I hope this works."

"So do I," John said to himself.

How long were they going to wait before they took a shot? John wondered.

A hundred yards. He could almost feel the sights of a rifle on him. He lowered himself until his head was directly behind Gent's neck.

The rocky spires and the stones stood out red and clear in the full blaze of sunlight. Behind the rocks, shadows. Movement.

He saw the snout of a rifle slide alongside one of the spires, its muzzle pointed straight at him.

"Now," John shouted and dug his spurs into Gent's flanks.

The horse rocketed beneath him and leaped into a full gallop, his head stretched out, ears flat, lips peeled back to brace the wind. John hugged the horse's neck, his head resting gently on its shoulder.

He drew his pistol, cocked it, held it tight against his leg. Below him, the ground blurred past. Beneath the pounding hoof-beats he could hear the thunder of his own heart, feel his throbbing pulse in his ears.

Next, he heard a loud *crack!*, like a bull-whip snapping the air.

Over his head, John heard the hiss of a bullet as it passed a foot above him.

Then there was another rifle shot and a bullet thudded into the earth below him, between Gent's legs, plowing a foot-long furrow before it struck a rock.

Out of the corner of his eye, he saw Ben and Dynamite, a half-length off to his left. Dynamite was tearing up the distance, eyes rolling wide open so that the whites gave him the look of madness.

Thirty yards they covered, John figured, then forty, and three rifles boomed in less than three seconds. A bullet sizzled past his ear like an angry hornet and his throat went dry. He looked toward the rocks and saw how close they were.

Repeating rifles, he thought. A Henry, maybe a couple of lighter Winchesters, all .44s, each bullet with enough lead to smash a man's heart to a pulp, flatten like a hammer when it struck bone, splintering a man's ribs into slivers.

The men behind the rocks stepped out, rifles at their shoulders.

John saw them, judged them to be less than thirty yards away. He raised his pistol, took aim, and fired at the man most in the open.

His bullet went wild, but all three men crouched and fired at him or at Ben.

He heard the bark of Ben's pistol and saw a chunk of rock break off one of the spires. There was a glimmer of red dust as some of the particles disintegrated into powder.

"Get the bastards!" a man shouted.

"Kill 'em," another yelled, jacking a cartridge into his rifle's firing chamber.

John swung his pistol on another man who had his rifle to his shoulder. He squeezed the trigger, felt the pistol buck in his hand.

Bullets whined as they skidded off rocks as Ben and John fired as fast as they could cock and pull the triggers of their pistols. The acrid smell of exploding gunpowder filled the air.

John knew he was ten or twelve yards from the rocks where the bushwhackers had waited for them.

Smoke wafted from the rifles and pistols.

He saw one of the men buckle as a bullet smashed into his midsection.

He heard a *thunk* and saw Ben's horse falter, stagger, and drop to its knees. Ben vaulted over the horse in a somersault and hit the ground, kicking up a cloud of reddish dust.

As one of the men swung his rifle to bear

on Ben, John shot him. He saw his head explode like a melon, spraying blood and brain mush onto one of the spires. The man went down like a sack of lead sash weights.

One rifleman still stood there, his body partially concealed behind a rock.

That man, Roscoe Bender, swung his rifle toward Savage and took deadly aim.

John reined in Gent, pulling the bit so tight he knew he must be cutting the horse's mouth. The horse skidded to a stop and John bailed out of the saddle.

The sky, the mountains, the rocks, and the land twisted in a blinding blur. All time seemed to stop on the brittle cusp of eternity. He felt his feet hit hard ground and a shock went through his body. His legs went numb as he waited for a .44 slug to blow out his brains and obliterate all thought, all memory, all breath, all precious, fleeting life.

15

Even though John's senses were scrambled, spinning like a whirligig, and his brain jolted off its axis, he brought his pistol up and leveled it at the head of Roscoe Bender.

"Mister, you either lower that rifle or I squeeze this trigger."

John knew it was a bold statement. The man's face was just a blur to him. The man had three heads, none of them in focus. But John held his front blade sight on the center image and it would take only a tick of his finger to bring the hammer down on a loaded .45 cartridge.

Bender's eyes narrowed. He looked at the pistol in Savage's hand. He saw the glitter of silver on the barrel, the rich bluing, the steady hand, the cocked hammer.

"You-you won't shoot me?" Bender stammered.

"Not if you lay your rifle down real quick."

John heard a groan from Ben, but he did

not look to see if his friend was all right. He concentrated on keeping his arm straight and steady and holding an unblinking gaze on the man with the rifle. He had no idea if the other two men were dead or alive.

Slowly, the rifle began to drop away from Bender's shoulder.

"Just let it drop to the ground, mister," John said. "Then step away."

Bender hesitated.

"I don't know if I can trust you," Bender said.

"I'm the only one you can trust. Better do it now. I got a hair trigger on this pistol and I just have to hiccup and you're a dead man."

Bender lowered the rifle another six inches.

John's jaw tightened and his eyes widened until they were as black as the twin barrels of a shotgun.

Bender eased the hammer down to half cock and dropped the rifle on the ground. Then he slung an arm up in front of his face to shield his eyes from the blazing sun at John's back.

"Now step away," John ordered. "I won't shoot you."

Bender took two steps away from the fallen rifle.

"That damned sun," Bender said.

John heard a low groan and his gaze shifted to one of the men on the ground. Kerrigan was doubled up, both hands holding his stomach. His hands were drenched with blood. He writhed in agony, his eyes closed against the glare of the sunlight.

"Who's that?" John asked.

"Name's Kerrigan."

"Your name?"

"Roscoe. Roscoe Bender."

"Who put you up to this, Bender?"

Bender did not answer.

John stepped closer to Bender. Roscoe's eyes were fixed on the pistol in Savage's hand.

"If you live long enough, you can give Ollie Hobart back whatever he paid you. Not that it'll do him any good. He's going to Boot Hill."

"Me, too, I reckon," Bender said.

John gave Bender a look of contempt. The man was wetting his pants.

"No, you're going to have to live with yourself awhile longer, Bender."

Ben was sitting up, holding his head with both hands.

"Cripes," Ben said, his voice a rasp in his throat.

"You all right, Ben?"

"I'll live, I reckon. Poor Dynamite. I think his leg's broke."

Ben crabbed over to his horse. Dynamite was lying on his side, holding a foreleg up. The leg and hoof were bloody. A black hole oozed blood just below his kneecap.

"You owe that man a horse, Bender. Maybe yours if he likes it. Where did you hide them?"

Bender pointed a thumb over his shoulder.

Kerrigan looked up at Savage with a cockeyed gaze. His hand slid away from his belly, crawled down to the butt of his pistol.

John swept his gaze away from Bender for a moment, fixed on Kerrigan.

"You won't live a second past the minute you touch the butt of that pistol," John said.

Kerrigan hesitated.

"Don't do it, Roy," Bender said, a tremor in his throat.

"I-I . . ." Kerrigan started to say, when a shudder rippled through his body. "I-I ain't dyin' . . ."

That was all he said. His right hand dropped to his pistol. He started to pull it from its holster. For being shot up as he was, he was pretty fast, John thought.

But not fast enough.

John's pistol moved like a striking snake.

The barrel swung on Kerrigan. John

squeezed the trigger, just a slight flick of his finger, and the hammer dropped. The pistol bellowed a deafening roar.

The .45 spit out sparks, a brief orange flame and seventy grains of lead. The pistol's recoil slammed into John's palm, but he held the barrel steady after the shot. He thumbed back the hammer so quick, the snick of the mechanism was muffled by the explosion.

Kerrigan ate the lead as it smashed through his teeth and into his mouth. Shards of teeth crumbled from his lips. The ball slammed into his spine at the back of his throat. There was an ugly smacking sound, the sound of bone breaking. He stiffened. His hand went slack and the pistol hung there, half out of its holster. His eyes glazed over with the final frost of death, fixed on a point just above John's head, and stared lifeless into eternity.

"Stranger, you don't think long on a thing, do you?" Bender said.

"I gave him fair warning," John said.

Ben got to his feet, stood on wobbly legs. The side of his face looked like raw meat where the stones and pebbles had ripped off hide. The red-streaked lines oozed droplets of blood.

"You did, at that," Bender said.

"You were hoping he was quicker than me, Bender. I could see it in your eyes."

"My eyes are plumb burned out from that sun. You took a chance riding in on us like that."

"Hard to look square at the sun and not go blind," John said.

"Lucky," Bender said.

Ben looked down at Dynamite. His feet were planted, but his upper body weaved like a snake charmer's cobra.

"John, look at Dynamite. I can see bone sticking out. His leg's plumb shattered. You gonna shoot that bastard or keep jawin' with him?"

Savage saw a shadow flicker in Bender's eyes. Bender swallowed and his Adam's apple made the skin on his throat quiver.

"You-you gave me your word, mister," Bender said, his voice pitched almost to a squeak.

"And what do you think my word's worth, Bender? What's yours worth?"

"Out here, that's about all a man's got, is his word, I reckon."

"And sometimes a man's word isn't worth a dollop of cowshit," Ben said. "That bastard ruined Dynamite. I got to put him down."

"I know, Ben," John said. "I'll do it for

you, if you want."

"No, damn it. I'll do it. I just don't like that feller standing there smug as a possum in a basket of persimmons while old Dynamite's got a busted leg."

"Bender's going to give you his horse, Ben. He's going to take us where he hobbled them. We'll have two more to sell."

"What about him?" Ben asked.

"He's going to walk back to Cheyenne and think about some things."

"What things?" Bender said, a quaver in his voice.

"You maybe might start with life and death, you sonofabitch."

Ben cradled Dynamite's head in his arms and put the pistol up to his left eye.

"So long, pard," Ben husked. "You been a good horse to me."

When the shot came, Bender and John both jumped. The report sounded like a cannon going off. Blood spurted from Dynamite's eye and peppered Ben's face so that it looked as if he had broken out with a severe case of measles. Tears streamed down his face and he gently let the horse's head down. Dynamite's high legs kicked out and twitched for a second or two. Then stopped.

"Jesus, Ben," John said. "I'm sorry as hell."

Ben stood up, wiped the blood on his

pistol barrel into the cloth of his trousers. He ejected the empty hulls and reloaded, holstered his pistol.

"Let's see about them horses," Ben said, his voice laden with gravel. "And then let's shoot this bastard's legs out from under him."

John looked at Ben as if seeing him for the first time.

"Ben, you ain't the killin' kind. Until now. What's changed?"

"I can't stand to see an animal suffer. 'Specially one I loved like a brother."

John understood. He knew how much Ben thought of Dynamite, about all horses and critters. He was softhearted. And to have to kill his own horse, that must have galled him beyond measure. Every man had his breaking point, he reckoned, and he had just seen Ben's.

Roscoe Bender was lucky to be alive.

Ben stripped Dynamite of his saddle, bridle, saddlebags, and bedroll. He tried not to look at his horse, but that was impossible. He stacked the gear behind the jumble of rocks.

"Ready?" John asked.

Ben nodded.

"Lead out, Bender. You so much as twitch, and you'll wind up like your friends. Take us to those horses you staked out for your bushwhack."

John walked alongside Ben, leading Gent.

"You want to ride, Ben? I don't mind walking."

"No. Them horses can't be far. Probably just out of sight of the road."

Bender didn't volunteer any information, but kept silent.

He led them to the horses, which all whickered when the three men hove into view.

"There they be," Bender said.

"You go on up and show me which horse is yours," John said.

Ben said nothing, but John could see that he was sizing up the three horses, perhaps choosing one that would suit him best.

"That four-year-old sorrel's my horse," Bender said. "Kerrigan rode that big chestnut gelding and Dooley's is the bay mare."

"Take your pick, Ben," John said.

"That chestnut looks pretty good," Ben said. He walked up to the horse, felt its chest, its legs, opened its mouth, and looked at its teeth. "He looks to be about five years old and sound. I reckon I'll ride him."

"The sorrel looks pretty good, too," John said.

"He'd wear out, I'm thinkin'," Ben said.

"And the mare, she's been rode hard and put away wet more'n once, I reckon."

"Those horses have names?" John asked.

"I don't know about Kerrigan's or Dooley's horses. I called mine Doofus."

Ben snorted.

"That's a hell of a name for a horse," Ben said.

"I don't ride him much," Bender said. "Bought him a year ago. He's tender-footed, I admit."

"Well, he ain't as tender-footed as you're going to be," Ben said. "Come on, John. Let's leave this bastard to the sun, the lizards, and the rattlesnakes."

"Hold Gent, will you, Ben?" John said. "I'll get those hobbles off and we can ride back and pick up your saddle. You want to switch, don't you?"

"Sure as hell," Ben said, glaring at Bender. Bender just stood there, a rueful look on his face.

John watched as Ben pulled himself into the saddle of the chestnut gelding. Ben rode him around in circles for a few minutes and then nodded to John.

John climbed onto Gent's back while holding the reins of the other two horses.

He looked at Bender.

"Don't bother walking back to those

rocks. You won't find any weapons there. You can keep that holster and the cartridges in your belt."

"You just going to leave me out here? It's a long walk back to Cheyenne."

"Call it mercy, Bender," John said.

He and Ben rode back toward the rocks. Neither of them looked back.

"I feel sorry for Bender," John said. "He could die of thirst before he reaches town on foot."

"That would suit me just fine," Ben gruffed. "The no-account bastard."

"You're a hard man, Ben," John said, a quirk of a smile on his face. "A lot harder than most."

"I learnt it from you, John Savage. Ain't no harder man than you, I reckon."

"I got my soft spots."

"Not so's you'd notice none. What you think is a splinter in your own eye looks like a big old log to me."

They gathered up the pistols and rifles, turned out the pockets of the dead men. Each kept the twenty dollars they found on Dooley and Kerrigan. Ben switched saddles, bridle, and saddlebags to the chestnut gelding and tied his bedroll on over the horse's rump.

"What're you going to call him, Ben?"

John asked when they had returned to the road and were heading north to Cheyenne.

"Haven't made my mind up, yet. I'm thinkin' on it. He steps out right lively, don't he?"

"The horse seems to suit you," John said.

"We'll see, Johnny. We'll see."

John knew one thing. Ben would never call the horse Dynamite, or anything close to it. He could see that Ben took the death of his horse hard. It was not an easy thing to get over, he knew.

It seemed to him that they rode with Death.

And all because of a man named Ollie Hobart.

Bender got off easy. He would show no such mercy to Hobart when he caught up with him.

He pictured Hobart dying real slow and real painful.

Maybe Ben was right, he thought. He was hard now. Whatever soft spot he had was slowly turning to rock.

16

Rosa Delgado was surprised when Ollie turned off the trail within spitting distance of Fort Laramie. She had fifty miles of dust on her face and clothes and longed for a hot bath and a soft bed.

"Where do we go?" she asked.

"See all those trees on that hill, off to our right?"

"I see them. But I do not see Fort Laramie."

"I'm meetin' Army and the boys up here, and maybe a scalper or two."

"A scalper?"

"Northern Cheyenne, maybe a Sioux."

"What do you do, Ollie?" There was a note of irritation in her voice. The sun was dropping in the west, daubing the clouds with soft pastels, plunging shadows into the recesses of the mountains. A pair of prairie swifts sliced through the air like feathered darts, winging their way to the thick stands

149

of pines atop the high knoll where they were headed.

"It is always the business first with you, eh, Ollie?"

"Always. The boys have a camp on the other side of that hill there. We won't stay long. I just want to see how things are going."

"What is it that you do with these men? You never did tell me."

"Maybe you'll find out when we meet up with them, Rosa. Just be patient."

"*Ay de mi, platica de paciencia, este hombre, pero anda de prisa todo el tiempo. 'Sus Mari . . .* I have the patience, Ollie. It is you who is always in the hurry."

Ollie laughed.

They circled the hill, then rode into shadow on the other side. Rosa could smell the scent of burning meat, the aroma of coffee. Yet she saw no smoke. Nor did she see any signs of a camp. Beyond, there was only prairie, desolate, forbidding.

Then she saw a man step from behind a tree. He was carrying a rifle. He raised an arm and waved to Ollie.

"There's Dick Tanner," Ollie said, waving back at the man.

"How do you find this place?" she asked. "And do the soldiers not know you have made the camp?"

"Now, Rosa. You ask too many questions. Just wait."

Dick Tanner stepped back into the trees. A moment later, Rosa heard a whistle that sounded almost like a prairie dog. They rode on until they were almost at the center of the hill when another man stepped into view. He beckoned to Ollie. Ollie turned his horse toward him. Rosa followed, her horse a half step behind his.

"Who is that?" she asked. "He does not look familiar to me. He looks *Indio.*"

"He is an Indian."

"Do you know him?"

"Yes. He's helping me on this business deal."

"What is this business deal?"

"Rosa, you jabber too much. Like a damned magpie. You'll find out soon enough."

She muttered a Mexican curse under her breath. His behavior had to do with his ancestry and the way he was conceived, she thought.

Blue Snake was from the Wind River Cheyenne tribe. He had been an army scout, but he had been fired because he drank too much, and on patrol he had been accused of leading troops in the wrong direction all too often. He was in his thirties, but the braided scar on his cheek, the broken nose, and the missing teeth made him look fifty. He was lean and wiry under his ill-fitting clothes and battered old cavalry hat. He wore a converted Colt Dragoon and carried a new Spencer carbine stolen from the armory at Fort Laramie.

"You come," he told Ollie.

Hobart and Rosa followed the ex-scout into the trees and along a game trail that encircled the hill. Rosa sniffed the heady scent of pines and listened to the soft pad of her horse's hoofs on brown pine needles. Blue Snake walked slowly and never looked back at them. His back was straight and his boot moccasins made no sound on the trail.

The outlaw camp was in a concealed clearing, midway up the small mountain. Trails led out in all directions, including one that led to a lookout atop the hill. When Ollie rode in, several armed men got to their feet. They curbed their enthusiasm, but Rosa had the feeling that they all wanted to cheer their leader.

"Howdy, boys," Ollie said, and swung down from his horse. "This here's Rosa and she's one of us. But she's not yours, she's mine, so keep your hands in your pockets and your peckers in your pants."

Army laughed, and so did the other white men. The three Indians showed no sign of emotion. But it was plain to Rosa that they recognized Ollie. Their black eyes flashed with recognition and she thought she detected a measure of respect.

"You took your sweet time getting here, Ollie," Army said. "We liked to have give up on you. Figured that pistolero with the fancy gun might have done you in."

"You don't have to worry about that little bastard no more," Ollie said.

"You rubbed him out?"

"I paid Roscoe to scratch him off my list when I hit Cheyenne."

Army grinned wide.

Ollie ignored him and walked over to one of the Indians. He and the two others wore white men's pants and shirts, moccasins, or scuffed work boots. A single braid snaked down from under his gray felt hat that was stained with grease and ground-in dirt. Both of the other Indians carried pistols in flapped army holsters and had new Spencer carbines lying close at hand next to them.

Ollie spoke, but also used his hands to make sign.

"Red Eagle. My heart is full to see you."

"How cola," Red Eagle said. He signed with

his hands and grunted low in his throat. "Make heap talk," he said in English. Then he looked at Rosa. "No squaw," he said.

Ollie turned to Rosa. "Red Eagle doesn't want you here, Rosa. Can you take a little walk?"

"Where?"

"Just someplace far enough away so's you can't hear none of us talkin'. Out of sight. Go sit under a tree or something."

"You let an *Indio* tell you what to do, Ollie? I will ride into Fort Laramie. I do not like you to treat me this way."

"You're not going into Fort Laramie. Now, just go sit someplace until this pow-wow is over."

Rosa's anger burned into her until her neck and cheeks turned vermilion. Her dark eyes blazed with fury. She balled up her fists.

"I take woman," Blue Snake said. He had been watching Ollie and Rosa and knew there was anger between them. "She sit. Me smoke."

"Rosa," Ollie said.

She looked at Blue Snake. He was a handsome man for an *Indio,* and he did not smell bad like most of them did. She nodded to him.

"I will go with Blue Snake," she said. "Maybe I will give him some whiskey."

"No whiskey," Red Eagle said, signing as well.

"I was making the joke. Maybe I will see what color is his snake."

Red Eagle looked puzzled. Blue Snake translated for him. His signing hands left no doubt as to Rosa's meaning.

Red Eagle and the other Indian both laughed.

Ollie scowled.

"You suit yourself, bitch," he said.

Rosa flashed him a savage look and took Blue Snake by the arm. Leading her horse, she walked off down one of the trails with him. The Lakota watched them and made obscene comments in their language, while Ollie tied his horse to a thin tree and sat down, glowering, his face dark as a thundercloud.

Army sat down, facing Ollie, a foot or two from Red Eagle.

"You better tell me what you know for sure, Army," Ollie said. "Not what you guess."

"You got a real tactful way of startin' up a palaver, Ollie. Downright heartwarmin'."

"I don't need your smart mouth, Mandrake. I just come off a long ride and my butt's sore as a neck boil. Red Eagle looks like he's been chewing ten-penny nails and

I don't see no sacks of gold lyin' about."

"Well, we got the rifles," Mandrake said. "Enough for Red Eagle's band. Tanner's keepin' a close eye on them miners up in the Medicine Bows. They outnumber the redskins. We're supposed to get more cartridges in a day or two."

"A day or two? How come?" Ollie speared Mandrake with a look sharp enough to draw blood.

"Quartermaster wants more money, Dick says."

"What about Fry?" Ollie asked.

Captain Jubal Fry was in charge of the armory. He had seen that the Winchesters were smuggled out of the fort. The quartermaster, Lieutenant Chester Newgate, was on Ollie's payroll, too. They all stood to make a great deal of money. But they were all nervous, as well.

"Jubal's a-workin' on it," Army said. "Chet's a damned peckerhead. He's featherin' his nest, holdin' up the whole deal."

"When can I see Fry?" Ollie asked.

"Later. This evening."

"What about the redskins? They still game?"

"Red Eagle says so."

"Me heap ready," Red Eagle said. "Many braves in camp. Good. Strong."

Red Eagle knew but a few English words. He understood even fewer, Ollie knew. Unless they spoke sign with him, he didn't understand most of what Ollie and his men talked about among themselves.

"Army," Ollie said, "can we trust these redskins?"

Mandrake shrugged.

"Long as you keep 'em away from the firewater, they seem like they want to clean out them miners. But I don't know. They're all pretty hard to read. When they jabber amongst themselves, you can't tell what they're thinkin'."

"They got to take blame for what we aim to do."

"I know. They don't mind."

"Good," Ollie said.

"Red Eagle says he can mount up twenty braves. Should be enough."

"I want to talk to Fry."

"He's supposed to meet us in town sometime after sundown," Army said.

"Where?" Ollie asked.

"The Hitchin' Post Saloon. Ain't nothin' but a little old cabin what used to be a store. They got some boards and barrels they use for a bar. They make their own whiskey and from what I hear, you drink enough of it you go blind and you get a headache like somebody beatin' on your head with ball-peen hammers."

"We'll take our own whiskey there."

Army grinned. "So Rosa's got some in her saddlebags, does she?"

"Army, do you think these red bastards mean to double-cross us?" Ollie spoke softly, keeping his gaze on Red Eagle. Ollie even smiled so that the Indian could not guess what his words meant.

"I think that bastard's got something up his sleeve. Oh, I think he means to keep his part of the bargain. But I think he and his braves have got a lot more on their minds than wiping out some gold diggers."

"Look at the bastard," Ollie said, his smile widening. "His eyes are as black as two piss holes in the snow. I wouldn't trust him as far as I could throw my horse."

"Don't worry. Me and Dick are going to keep a close eye on that bird."

"Maybe he ain't the onliest one who's got plans for afterward," Ollie said.

"What do you mean?" Mandrake asked.

Ollie took his gaze away from Red Eagle and looked straight at Army.

"Redskins with carbines make me mighty damned nervous," he said.

Mandrake's throat went dry as his hands broke out in a clammy sweat. He was thinking that they were sitting down with the Devil, and the trail to the gold stretched a long way from that little mountain where they were all hiding out, waiting for everything to come together. He didn't say anything to Hobart, but he was wondering if Red Eagle understood a lot more English than he owned up to.

When he looked at Red Eagle, there were those piercing eyes, black as a pair of gun barrels, and no sign of what was going on behind them in that savage brain.

17

The noon sun, a pale yellow cauldron shimmering with lashing fire, blazed down on Cheyenne when Ben and John rode in, leading two saddled horses. Several people on the street eyed them with suspicion, then hurried to their destinations. One man who didn't look away or turn tail and scurry off sat on a large nail keg outside a hardware store. John rode up to him, with Ben following.

"Howdy, mister," John said. "I'd like a little information."

"Howdy to you, stranger. What kind of information?"

The man wore a faded pair of overalls, smoked a corncob pipe, and sported a grizzled beard that was streaked brown and red to match the hair that spewed from under his battered felt hat. John could smell the tobacco smoke from a dozen feet away. It bore the fragrance of freshly cut apples.

An old woman wearing a large sunbonnet walked up to a pump, carrying a wooden pail. She bent down and worked the handle up and down until water flowed from the spout. She held the bucket under it and shooed away a dog that trotted up, rib bones showing through its yellow hide.

"We got some horses and saddles to sell," John said, "and don't want to answer a lot of questions."

"I see. You horse thieves?"

"You got a blunt manner to you, mister."

"Blunt gets right down to the nub of things, don't you think? Now, if you want to pussyfoot around, maybe you oughta ask somebody else about selling them horses."

The man pulled a toothpick out of his shirt pocket and started poking it between a pair of top teeth. The yellow dog trotted by, looked up at the man, then tucked its tail between its legs and scooted off. The old woman walked away from the pump, water sloshing in her pail. Her ankles were swollen from arthritis and her sunbonnet brim flopped up and down as a gust of wind rivered down the street. Her dress billowed out and then sagged back to her plump frame like a collapsing tent.

"Well, sir, they's the stables. But that one horse belongs to old Roscoe Bender, and I doubt he sold it to you. Don't know who them other two belonged to, but I seen 'em around. You might have bought 'em and you might not have."

"You can sure talk a man's ear off, all right. But you don't give out any information, old-timer. I'm short on both time and patience, but if you have someone in mind to buy a couple of horses and some firearms, I'd be mighty obliged if you were to tell me of such a man."

"You ain't from around here, I reckon."

"No."

"But you're already engaged in some sort of commerce 'thout knowin' who to deal with."

"You're some philosopher, I'll grant you that," John said.

"Ain't philosophy. I'm a studier on human nature. You boys don't look much like horse thieves or owlhooters, but you got one questionable horse there and two others I seen around. Now let me see. Who might pay for such 'thout askin' a whole lot of questions?"

The man slid his hat back on his head and made a show of scratching his head as if he were studying on a real puzzler of a question. But John already knew that there was such a man, there always was in every town, and that this cantankerous old blabber-mouth knew just who it was. So he waited while the scratching went on and then finished up.

"You could take 'em over to the livery stables, but that's where Roscoe keeps that horse. Maybe them other two boards up there, too."

"I'm just about to shoot those two saddle horses I got and leave them here so you can clean up the mess," John said.

"Well, now, that'd be a shame to kill two good horses just for spite."

"That sun's mighty hot. We're tired and we're hungry, so I'd do just about anything to speed up this conversation. If you have any information, I'd be mighty glad to get it. You want a commission on the sale, is that it?"

The man laughed and slapped his knee.

"No, sirree, sir, I'm not a commission man. Just an old boy puttin' in his time on this good earth. You might want to ride down here a few blocks to Juniper Street, turn right, and go to the edge of the prairie. They's a little log house yonder and some corrals, a kind of fleabag tradin' post what's owned by a gent goes by the name of Lenny Renfrew. He buys and sells all sorts of junk and he's likely there now, just waitin' for two dust-covered horse traders like yourselves to show up and make him an offer."

"I thank you kindly, mister," John said. "Now, do you want a couple of dollars for your trouble?"

"Nope. I done did all my drinkin' in my youth and I got plenty of grub in the larder. I generally see everybody what rides through here and gets my satisfaction in tryin' to figger out where they come from and where they be a-goin'."

"We don't offer that kind of information to strangers," John said.

Behind him, Ben snorted. He had been enjoying the exchange, but now he mopped his brow with an already soggy bandanna and tapped his new horse in the flanks, ready to move on.

The man cackled and waved the toothpick at John.

"You be careful, son. If you stay in Cheyenne, look out you don't get skinned. Ain't everybody here as kindly as me."

"I'll keep that in mind. Thanks again for the directions."

"You watch out for Lenny. He's one what will skin you if you ain't careful. He might not be as bad as some of the fat politicians we got here, but he'll do until one of them rascals comes along."

"If the town's so full of skunks, how come you live here?" John asked, drawn to the taciturn man somehow.

"Hell, I helped build this town. Worked on the railroad. Crew boss said this was as good a place as any for a town, so they started drivin' stakes. Hell, it warn't a bad place before the shysters and the no-accounts come in. Still ain't a bad place, considering some other towns I been in back in my time."

"Well, good luck to you, mister," John said.

"Don't need none."

"How's that?" John asked.

"Luck's what you need when you ain't got brains. I still got them. And I don't gamble or drink hard likker, so don't need a bit of luck, good or bad."

"Suit yourself," John said.

"Yair, well, that's what I generally do, young feller. You mind your business with Lenny, and you'll come out all right."

"John, let's get on over there," Ben said. The horses were restless, pawing the ground with their hooves, switching their tails at flies, tossing their manes.

"Yeah, Ben. So long, old-timer."

The old-timer lifted a hand, but he said

not a word. Ben and John rode off to find Lenny.

"That old feller," Ben said, "you and him seemed to get along."

"I didn't think so."

"Notice anything, ah, peculiar about him?"

"His orneriness, I reckon."

"Nope, that ain't it."

"What is it, then?"

"He reminded me of your pa."

"My pa? Hell, he doesn't look anything like my pa."

"Nope, he don't look like him, but he sure acts like him. Talks like him, too."

"I didn't see it," John said.

"Well, I thought I was listenin' to your pa back there. Come back to life."

John started to shake his head, then thought about the old man. Ben had a point. His father had been a man of few words. And Daniel Savage had been a good judge of character, just like the old-timer. He tried to put his father's face on the old man, but it didn't work. Yet, when he recalled the conversation, he allowed that Ben was probably right. Dan didn't waste words and he could size a man up better than most. He had picked a pretty good bunch to go mining with him.

"You got a lot of them same qualities, Johnny," Ben said. "Every day, I keep thinkin' you get to lookin' and soundin' like your pa."

"Aww."

"It's true," Ben said.

If that were so, John thought, it wasn't deliberate. He had never tried to look or act like his father. But he supposed some things rubbed off from father to son. He couldn't see it himself, but he knew Ben paid attention to such things. He studied people. He was a good poker player. He read books and he spent time alone, thinking. Which was something John had never fully understood. At times, Ben would go off by himself to smoke, and sometimes John would join him and they would talk about things they never spoke of in camp with the other men, or with his parents. He held Ben in high respect, mostly because of those times when they had talked together about books and philosophy, nature, the universe itself.

Lenny's ramshackle house looked like a junkyard. There were parts of buggies, leaf springs, axles, wheels, wagon tongues, even weathered oxen yokes lying about like the wreckage from a wagon train, many of the metal parts rusted and broken, seemingly of no use to anyone.

There was a sign propped up against one end of the porch. The sign was old, weather-beaten, the paint faded and scoured by wind and rain. It read: HORSES BOUGHT & SOLD. SADDLES. TACK. BRIDLES. FEED. They could see a pole corral out back, a fenced pasture and loose shingles on both sides of the house. A man sat on the sagging front porch smoking a clay pipe, a bottle of whiskey sitting next to his rocking chair. He had some leather traces spread across his lap along with a leather punch and a mallet.

Ben and John rode up close. John looked down at the man, who cocked his head and removed the pipe from his mouth.

"You Lenny?" John asked. "Lenny Renfrew?"

"I might be. Who's askin'?"

"We have some horses and saddles to sell."

"You got bills of sale?"

"No," John said.

"Hmm. Well, since I know the owners of three of those horses you're riding, I might ask them to verify they sold 'em to you."

"Two of the former owners are no longer with us," John said. "As for Roscoe Bender's horse, we made a trade."

"Oh?"

168

"Yes. He killed my friend's horse and we took his. Fair trade, wouldn't you say?"

"Is Roscoe still among the living?"

Ben laughed.

"He's among the tenderfeet," John said.

"What the hell's that supposed to mean?" Renfrew said.

"That mean's Roscoe Bender is afoot, walking back to Cheyenne. It'll take him the rest of the day, easy. Anyway, we're not selling his horse. That should make it simple for you."

"I dunno," Renfrew said.

"Well, I'll make it easy for you," John said, drawing his pistol. He put the barrel up against the head of one of the outlaw horses, cocked it. "I can just drop both of them right here. You're welcome to the meat and the leather on them."

Renfrew shot out of his chair like a jumping jack on springs. He stretched out his arms in protest.

"Hell, don't do that," he said. "We can deal. What you want for the whole kit and caboodle?"

John eased the hammer back down and lowered his pistol. He did not put it back in its holster.

"That's better," John said.

"I can see you boys mean business," Renfrew said.

"You don't know the half of it, Mr. Renfrew. Those two who owned these horses, along with good old Roscoe Bender, tried to kill us. They drygulched us south of town. They were hired by a man I'm hunting. A man who killed my folks and a whole lot of other people, robbed them of their gold."

"Who might that be?" Renfrew said, stepping gingerly off the porch as if he were walking on uncracked eggs.

"A man named Ollie Hobart."

Renfrew's face drained of color, turned a sickly pale hue as if he had been kicked in the nuts.

"Ollie Hobart?"

"That's right. If he's still in town, I aim to raise the population of your cemetery."

"Ollie's bad medicine, mister. But maybe you know that."

"Yeah. He leaves a terrible taste in my mouth, Mr. Renfrew. Now, do we deal or not? We don't have all day."

"No, I reckon not. I don't know where Hobart is. I ain't seen him in months. But I heard talk that he had some doings in Fort Laramie. Man at the saloon come through here headed that way. Name of Army Mandrake. A man as bad as they come, from what I hear."

"A hundred dollars for both horses, saddles, bridles, the works," John said.

"Done," Renfrew said without hesitation. His hands were shaking when he took the reins from Ben. They were still shaking when John slid his pistol back in its holster and held out his hand for the money.

A small cloud drifted between the earth and the sun. Ben looked up, squinting against the glare.

When Renfrew counted out the money and handed it to John, Ben knew that the brief shade was as good as it was going to get for them that day.

18

Hobart felt uncomfortable. He didn't like being out in the open, so close to the fort. There were so many people around, he and his men were bound to draw attention to themselves. He was sure Mandrake had taken every precaution, but the campsite had served its purpose. It was time to move.

"Army, how long you been here?" Ollie asked.

"Three days."

"You get a place in town like I asked you?"

"Sure did."

"Tell me about it."

Mandrake scooted over closer to Hobart. He stuck a cheroot between his lips, but didn't light it. Overhead, streamers of small clouds were changing color as the sun fell away toward the west. He glanced up, worked the cheroot from one side of his mouth to the other, and began talking.

"It's out of the way, over on the high end

of town. Furnished. Owned by a little old lady who thinks I'm a drummer. Lost her husband some twenty years ago. Snake bite, I think. Rent's cheap. No neighbors. Got a stove, plenty of wood for cold nights, a good well. Made out of logs. It's even got some old gun ports that someone filled with mud and plastered over. They can be knocked out real quick."

"What about a place in the Medicine Bows?"

"Me'n Tanner found a good place, near where them prospectors are workin'. Plenty of cover, a little spring, completely out of sight of the road. Hard to get to. No signs of anyone bein' there. We come up on it from the back side. Didn't make no blazes, just used landmarks to make it easy to get to. We been there twice since and nobody's even come close."

"Good."

Hobart looked over at the Indians. They were talking in low voices among themselves. He didn't trust them. He had known Red Eagle for some years, Blue Snake even longer. But times had changed. Circumstances had changed. These men belonged on reservations, but they danced the ghost dance and believed they would one day recover their lands and all the white men would be dead or driven back into the sea.

"Does Fry know about the place in town?" Ollie asked.

"He's the one what told me about it."

"What about Chet Newgate?"

"I don't know. Maybe. Lieutenant Newgate acted real funny last time I talked to him. Like he wanted to wash his hands of the whole deal. I wanted some supplies for the redskins and he turned me down."

"Does he want more money? Is that it?" Ollie asked.

"I asked him that. He just shook his head. Said he didn't have none of what we wanted. I told Cap'n Jubal Fry about it, askin' if he could have a talk with Newgate."

"And what did Fry say?"

"Said he'd look into it."

"And did he?"

"Ain't heard back since. But he didn't act surprised. He mumbled somethin' but when I asked him what he was sayin', he just changed the subject."

"I don't like none of it, Army. Do we have enough guns for the redskins?"

"I dunno. Red Eagle says he has twenty more braves that need rifles and pistols. I told him I wanted to see 'em, and he looked at me like I was a bug or somethin'."

"Where in hell would he get twenty more

braves? I think the bastard's lyin'," Hobart said.

"Me, too. And I don't trust Fry no more, neither."

"Fry is the key to this whole deal. He's supposed to keep the army off our asses when we jump them miners up in Dead Horse Canyon."

"I wouldn't count on that no more."

"Is there something else you need to tell me, Army? Anything you're holdin' back?"

"I think we ought to go ahead with what we got and to hell with the soldier boys."

Hobart scratched his chin, closed his eyes for a second, then waved a hand in the air. Army waited for some comment on his suggestion, but Hobart just bunched up his lips and shook his head as if in doubt.

"Go get Dick back here. I'll get Rosa. Let's get the hell out of here. Tell Red Eagle we'll meet up with him tomorrow night."

"Where? He can't come into town."

"His camp in the Medicine Bows."

"You know where it is, Ollie?"

"Yeah. It's a lot safer than this one. I'll talk to Blue Snake, see if I can tell which way the wind's blowing."

"I don't trust that buck," Mandrake said.

"I don't trust Red Eagle. Not anymore."

Mandrake swore, got to his feet. He

started walking to the lookout post where Dick Tanner was standing guard. Ollie signed to Red Eagle, telling him to wait for him. He stood up and walked off in the direction he had sent Rosa and Blue Snake.

Blue Snake was pulling on a bottle of whiskey from Rosa's Cantina when Ollie walked into the small clearing. Rosa sat nearby, her skirt hiked up high, nearly to her thighs. She wore a wicked smile on her face.

Ollie walked up to Blue Snake, jerked the bottle from his hands, and drove a fist into his face. Blue Snake's eyes rolled in their sockets. Blood squirted from his nose and mouth. He fell to one side as if he were poleaxed.

Ollie turned to Rosa.

"Pull your skirt down, you whore," he said to her.

"You do not order me," she said, glaring at him with dark, malevolent eyes.

"Rosa, you've just about wore out your welcome. You want to lie with the bucks, I'll sell you to Red Eagle. He sure as hell would be a hero if he took you back to his camp and turned you over to his bucks."

"You would not do such a bad thing," she said.

"You drunk?"

"No. I gave the Indian a swallow, that is all. It is hot and I was cooling my legs."

She pulled her skirt down and stood up, brushed herself off.

"You know what firewater does to Injuns, Rosa."

"I know."

"It makes 'em mean. Makes 'em want to go on the warpath. You ought to know better."

"You leave me alone with this *Indio*. I am not good enough for you to keep me by your side when you talk. I give the *Indio* a drink. What is so bad about that?"

Ollie walked over to her, drew his arm back, and slapped her on the cheek. She gasped and staggered backward. Her hand went to her face. Tears filled her eyes. She opened her mouth. He clamped it shut.

"You scream, Rosa, or you say one damned word and I'll beat you to within an inch of your life and leave you to the buck. Now get on your horse. We're ridin' out of here."

Ollie took his hand away. Rosa wiped the tears from her face with her sleeve.

"Wh-where do we go?" she asked.

"Into town. But you're on a short leash, Rosa. You got that?"

"You are a cruel man, Ollie Hobart," she said.

"Rosa, you don't know what mean is yet."

There was a dirty towel on the ground. Ollie stooped over, picked it up, and wrapped the whiskey bottle in it. He put the bottle back in Rosa's saddlebag as she was untying her horse's reins from a small juniper bush. Then he walked over to Blue Snake, grabbed him by the braid, and jerked the brave to his feet.

"No drink firewater," he said to Blue Snake.

Blue Snake just glared at him.

"Go back," Ollie said, gesturing toward the camp.

Blue Snake dropped a hand to the butt of his pistol.

"You draw that pistol, Blue, I'll gut you like a fish."

The Indian's eyes narrowed, then widened. But he dropped his hand away from his pistol and started walking back to the camp.

"*Un dia,*" Rosa muttered under her breath, "*voy a cortar sus juevos de su cuerpo y tirar a los puercos.*" Ollie didn't hear her, and if he did, he wouldn't have understood the Spanish. She had said that one day she would castrate him and throw his balls to the hogs.

■ ■ ■ ■

Camp was breaking up when they got back. Army had returned with Dick Tanner, and the Indians were retrieving their horses.

"I'm glad to get out of here," Tanner said. "I got dents in my back from sleepin' on rocks. Army says we're going into town."

"Soon as that sun sets," Ollie said. "And we're going in separate-like. Not in a bunch. Dick, you take Rosa to the hideout. I'll ride in with Army since he knows the way."

Dick pulled himself into the saddle. Ollie mounted up.

"What did you do to Blue Snake?" Army asked.

"I weaned him from the whiskey," Ollie said, darting an angry glance at Rosa. She turned her head away from him.

The sun had set behind the mountains. Long shadows painted the land, puddled up under trees. A cool wind sprang up, riffled through the pines, dislodging cones that fell soft atop the brown pine needles. The blue drained from the sky in the east and the high clouds turned pale pink, with edges bright as smelted silver.

"I go with Tanner?" Rosa asked.

"Yes," Ollie replied.

"Where do we go? To a hotel?"

"A house," Ollie said. "You just do what Dick says. Dick, if she gives you any trouble, knock her in the head with the butt of your pistol."

"Aw, Ollie, she's a woman."

"Don't argue with me, Dick. She was about to let Blue Snake put the boots to her."

"Do not talk about me like that, Ollie," Rosa said. "I am a good woman."

"We'll see about that, Rosa. Now git, the both of you."

He watched as Rosa and Dick took one of the paths down to the flat. Soon, they disappeared. Ollie and Army were alone.

"You shouldn't have brought that Mex with you, Ollie. She's already trouble. I smelled whiskey on Blue Snake's breath. Whiskey and blood where you broke his nose. I think you maybe got an enemy there."

"Where did you get the idea that any of these redskins weren't my enemy, Army?"

"I dunno. You been friends with Red Eagle a long time."

"Army, I ain't got no friends. And if I did, it wouldn't be no red nigger."

"Yeah," Army said. He pulled himself into the saddle.

The clouds were turning to ash in a dusky sky. The wind stiffened.

"You ready to ride in, Ollie?" Army asked.

"Just take it slow. After we get to the hideout house, I want you to send Tanner in to get Fry and Newgate out there. We got to have a serious powwow or this whole operation's going to turn to shit."

A jay squawked somewhere in the pines and there were dark holes in between the trees. A solemnity settled over the land. By the time they reached the flat, it was dark and quiet.

Like a graveyard.

19

Ben cut into his steak as if preparing to dine on his last meal. Watery blood trickled onto his plate from the partially done center of the meat. He forked a bite into his mouth and chewed it until it was small enough to swallow.

"I almost heard that one moo when you touched a knife to it, Ben," John said.

"I like my beef almost raw."

"To grow hair on your chest?"

"You could use a little on yours, sonny."

"I like my meat cooked. It's what separates me from the savage animal."

"Nothing separates you from the savage animal, Johnny."

"Let's not whistle that tune again, Ben."

John stabbed a cluster of string beans and dropped them into his mouth.

The Chaparral Café was not crowded at that hour. Two men sat at a side table against the wall; two women chatted at one near the back. Ben and John sat near the middle and felt the heat from the wood stove that was set against the other wall, behind a small counter. A Mexican woman had waited on them and now sat at the counter, saying her beads, while the cook, a skinny Mexican in his twenties, added boiling water to a sink full of plates, cups, eating utensils, a fry pan, and some bowls. A fly roamed its buzzing path overhead, finally landing on the ceiling.

"Well," Ben said, "you got the name, anyways."

"John?"

Ben chuckled.

"I was thinking of Savage," he said.

"Well, you always were slow, Ben," John cracked.

Ben cut another chunk of steak, sawing it into a bite-sized square, and stuffed it into the corner of his mouth. John drank a swallow of warm beer, then cut into a boiled potato.

The waitress finished her silent recitation and slipped the rosary into the pocket of her apron. One of the women at the back table called to her.

"Elena, more tea, please."

"Chure," Elena said. *"Un momento."*

The other two men slurped soup from a

pair of bowls. One dabbed a flour tortilla onto his plate, soaked it with juices, and popped it into his mouth. They looked like brothers, were in their thirties, and wore homespun shirts, work boots, and faded denims. They spoke in English, talked about some girls they knew. The fly paid them a visit and one of them swatted the air in front of his face.

John was eating fast; he kept looking out the front window.

Ben chewed his steak slowly, his back to the street.

"We could maybe stay the night and rest up, Johnny. With that extry money you got from the horse sale."

"No, we'll go on."

"Shit fire, John. Can't some things wait a damned day?"

"Some things can. Laundry, currying, a good foot soak."

"You don't give up, do you?" Ben said.

"Not on important things. Every minute Hobart draws a breath is a minute too long for me."

"Revenge is a dish best served cold."

"Mine is already too cold, Ben. Finish that steak and let's make some miles before sundown."

"I'd like to air out my sweaty old bedroll,

184

sleep on a soft mattress tonight."

"Me, too."

"But you won't."

"We'll find us bunks in Fort Laramie," John said.

"That a promise, Johnny?"

John nodded, finishing off his steak. The fly landed in a puddle of spilled beer. Ben brought a glass down on top of it, mashing the fly into a squish of blood and goo.

Within the half hour, the two men were riding out of Cheyenne, heading for Fort Laramie. The sun had slid from its zenith and was now burning their faces and eyes. They pulled their hat brims down and hunched over their pommels, the horses swatting at deer flies like a pair of hairy metronomes. *Swick, swish, swick, swish.* The gray flies drew blood on both Ben's and John's arms. The stings were just another series of annoyances among many as the summer sun boiled the beer out of their flesh, leaving a residue of attractants for the murderous deer flies.

The road was well traveled and they passed numerous roads branching off to unknown parts — ranches, prospecting sites, other towns; they did not know. They nodded to people heading for Cheyenne,

185

families, single riders, couples on wagons or pulling carts with burros. Toward late afternoon, the traffic thinned out and they rode across a quiet deserted land where hawks flew over broken country, their shadows rippling over rocks and uneven ground. Prairie swifts darted in pairs toward the east and buzzards floated high in the sky, whirling slowly in circles with only an occasional flap of wings.

"A man could get mighty lonesome in this country," Ben said as the sun blazed at them head-on in its slow slide to the western horizon.

"It makes a man think," John said. "Makes him feel mighty small."

"Oh, I felt small when we was up in the mining camp," Ben said. "All them mountains loomin' over our heads. But it's different out here. The mountains don't seem so big, but the land, it just swallers up a man. Like there ain't no end to it."

"It's a bigger country than I ever imagined, all right," John said.

"Sometimes, when they're ain't no people about, none on the road, and all, it feels like we're the onliest ones still alive. Like somethin' come along and swept all the people away, blew the towns to dust. All that sage and chaparral, lizards and snakes, turkey buzzards and hawks. This ain't no place for people, I'm thinkin'."

"People live here."

"Where?"

"Off in the mountains or on the plain, I reckon."

Ben shuddered, as if he had been struck by a sudden chill.

"Why would a man want to live out here?"

"Some folks like it quiet and peaceful, Ben. I don't mind it. And out on the prairie a man can see a long ways. In every direction. Might be some comforting to a lot of folks."

"Not to me. I got to know there's a house over the next hill, with people in it, some stock grazin', a pond with catfish in it, and roads goin' by with people wavin' as they pass."

"You better move back East, then, Ben. You'd go plumb crazy out here."

Suddenly, Ben straightened in the saddle and peered straight ahead. He tried shading his eyes, but he was staring straight into the sun.

"Damn," he said. "I thought I saw somethin' up ahead yonder."

"What?"

"I dunno. Dust. Road twists and all them little buttes and such, it's hard to see a long way down this road."

John looked.

He thought he saw a shift in the light, a haze where the sun shot small rays in every direction. The sun was blinding, but he looked off to the side and thought he saw a dust cloud wafting easterly, reddish and yellow and amber, like whiskey in a cut glass when the light strikes it just right.

"It isn't anything," John said, but he didn't sound too sure of himself.

"A lot of dust, looks like."

"Ben, I've been seeing lakes and ponds and tall oak trees all afternoon. The light plays tricks on you."

"Maybe. But that's a lot of dust for nothin'."

"Cattle running, maybe."

John saw that there was more dust than before, a larger cloud. It looked thicker toward the ground and then almost vaporous as it rose in the air.

"Look at Gent's ears, John."

John saw Gent lift his head. His ears were twisting like weather vanes in the wind. His nostrils were distended as if he were sniffing the air, trying to pick up a scent.

"Maybe he sees that dust, too," John said.

"Hell, it's getting closer. Buffalo?"

"I don't know. Could be. If so, we're right

in their path."

"Maybe we ought to ride off, way off, just in case."

"Let's wait awhile, see if we can make out what's raising all that dust."

John stood up in the stirrups. There was a lot of dust now. He could see it plain. Getting closer. His forehead knitted in thought. If a herd of buffalo was stampeding, they were sure in the way. They could be trampled unless they could ride away, outrun them.

"Can't see a thing, damn it," Ben said. "Just a whole lot of dust."

"Look away for a minute. Then, just look at the road, see if you can see anything moving toward us."

"Good idea."

Ben looked off to the side. So did John. John closed his eyes for a moment, then opened them again. There wasn't any dust anywhere else but straight ahead. And no wind to speak of. Just a light zephyr blowing down from the mountains.

"It's dust all right. Stirred up by animals or people. But it's not moving fast."

"What do you mean?"

"I mean it doesn't look like something stampeding. Maybe a bunch of wagons or riders."

"Could be, I reckon," Ben said.

They rode on and the dust seemed to vanish only to rise up again, closer.

"I-I think I see somethin'," Ben said after a few minutes had passed by.

John narrowed his eyes and stared down the road, just below where the sun hung like a pale buttercup above the horizon.

Movement. Little dark specks. Dust spooling out behind whatever it was. Wider than the road. A puzzling sight just then, he thought.

"I see something, too," John said. "Riders? Men on horseback?"

"Too far to tell just yet."

Ben stood up in the stirrups to give himself a longer view. His horse snorted and switched its tail, flapping at deer flies.

A few more minutes passed by as the two men rode more slowly down the road. John was ready to spur Gent and turn him off to the west or even double back, if need be. He felt his muscles tauten and tingle with an electric surge that always came when there was danger.

"I see 'em," Ben said. "They are riders, a whole passel of 'em. I count eight, no nine, no, maybe a dozen or so. Headin' straight for us."

John saw them, too. They were fanned out,

some on the road, some flanking either side of it. They rode in perfect formation as if they were after something he could not see. They were twenty or thirty yards apart. The horses were not running, but they were at a brisk walk, perhaps a trot, and they were kicking up dust.

The sun glinted off metal until it appeared as if the riders were setting off silver sparks of light that winked like stars shining in the daylight.

"Hell," Ben said. "Them are soldiers. I can see their uniforms. Ever' damn one of 'em is dressed the same. And look, one of 'em's holding a flag of some sort."

"A guidon," John murmured, recognizing the yellow-and-blue pennant that flapped like a broken wing.

"I wonder what they're after," Ben said. "Injuns?"

The troop of soldiers drew closer. John could see their hats and their faces. They were following a man with bars on his shoulders. They made a V and were coming at him like a human spear. He saw their gloves, then, the glistening hides of their horses, horses that were all the same color. The men all carried rifles, and he saw that they were wearing sidearms.

"No, Ben, not Indians," John said, slow-

191

ing Gent to a halt. "Pull up."

"What? Why? What are they huntin' all spread out like that?"

John let out a breath as Gent stopped, held steady, his muscles quivering at the sight of all those horses.

"From the looks of them, it's a patrol. And it sure looks like they're comin' for us."

Ben stopped his horse alongside John.

The soldiers were less than four hundred yards away. There was a flash of light as one of the soldiers, riding alongside the leader, pulled a pair of binoculars down from his eyes.

"What makes you think they're comin' for us, John?" Ben asked.

John looked at Ben.

"Because we're the only ones out here," he said.

And then he could smell the dust as the breeze changed direction. It smelled of horse sweat and man sweat, sage and chaparral. It smelled of ancient wars and warriors, and it clung to his nostrils like the cloying smell of death.

20

The lieutenant, who was leading the cavalry troop, drew his pistol and aimed it straight at John.

"You hold up right there," he shouted. "Get your hands up."

Ben's hands went up first. John slowly raised his arms and waited.

Soldiers swarmed around them, some with drawn pistols, others aiming Spencer rifles at Ben and John.

The lieutenant hauled up on his reins and stopped his horse beside Gent, so that he was staring straight into John's eyes.

"Identify yourself," the lieutenant snapped.

Before John could answer, one of the troopers reached over and jerked John's rifle from its scabbard. Another pulled his pistol from its holster. Soldiers did the same with Ben.

Off in the distance, a hawk voiced its piping *scree, scree* as it sailed over the bronzed land.

"I'm John Savage."

"And you," the lieutenant said, shifting his gaze to Ben.

"Benjamin Russell."

The lieutenant looked Ben and John over, his eyes as cold and pale blue as arctic ice at dusk. He was military trim, with no facial hair, his sideburns razor cut. His uniform was covered with a patina of dust, like those of the men under his command. There was dust on all their faces, as well, and their hands and faces were burnished dark from days in the sun and wind.

"Where are you from?" the lieutenant asked.

"That's hard to say," John said. "Why do you ask?"

"Mister, you answer and answer quick. I don't have to give you a reason and I'm not going to."

"We come up from Coloraddy," Ben said. "Before that . . ."

"Ben, you don't have to answer this man," John said. "And, sir, you have no right to hold us at gunpoint and take our weapons. I demand that you give them back and leave us be. We're civilians."

One of the troopers edged his rifle closer

to John. There was no mistaking the threat.

"This is a military district, mister," the lieutenant said. "We have the right to detain you, and that's just what we're going to do. Sergeant Dillard, put these men in irons."

Sergeant Dillard nodded to two other men, who rode up and produced handcuffs.

"Put your hands behind your backs," Dillard ordered.

Ben did as he was told.

John reached out for the nearest trooper and grabbed him by the throat. Dillard rode up, pistol in hand, and clubbed John on the back of the head. Hard. John slumped in the saddle. One of the troopers wrestled John's hands behind his back and slipped on handcuffs, tightened them until the rings bit into John's skin.

"Wake him up," the lieutenant ordered. He saw that Ben was cuffed and nodded to Dillard.

"Let's move out. Back to the fort."

They rode into the sunset. Four troopers flanked John and Ben. Two others held the reins of their horses. They rode into the night, flankers out, scouts riding point under a starry sky, the Milky Way a carpet of strewn diamonds, the moon just a sliver above the horizon.

John's head hurt where the sergeant had

clubbed him. The lump throbbed like a second beating heart. Each pulsing drum of it sent a shot of pain through his head, down his neck, and into his spine.

The cavalry did not stop for two hours. Then the lieutenant called a halt so that the men could relieve themselves and the horses could rest.

"I'm Lieutenant Herzog," he said to John. "I will let you down to relieve yourself, but if you try to escape, one of my men will open up that goose egg on your pate. You got that?"

"Yeah."

"That's 'yes, sir,' to you, Savage."

John did not reply.

Herzog spoke to one of the troopers watching John.

"Tim, you get him down out of the saddle and let him pee. Give him some water if he wants any."

"Yes, sir," Trooper Tim Bullock said. He dismounted and helped John out of the saddle. He walked him out into the dark, away from the horses and other men.

"Are you going to hold it for me, Tim?" John asked, a sarcastic edge to his voice.

"No, sir, I'm going to loosen one cuff and you can hold it your damned self."

John saw Ben taking a leak a few yards away. Ben was tired, he knew, and probably cursing the soldiers under his breath. *Probably me, too,* he thought.

When John was finished, Tim said to him, "Sir, I got to buckle you back up. Sorry."

"Do you know what this is all about? Why we're being detained?" John asked.

"No, sir. I think we were chasing some bad men. The colonel at the fort, he said to bring in anybody who looks suspicious."

"Do I look suspicious?"

"No, sir, I reckon not. But we got orders."

The patrol reached the fort late that same evening. Pickets allowed them to pass onto the parade ground. John was surprised that there was no high fence around the fort. Instead, it sprawled over a wide area, looked more like a village than an army fort. He had expected there to be a stockade, riflemen walking the ramparts. For several moments he thought there must be some mistake, that the men he had ridden with were not really soldiers, and they were not at Fort Laramie but in some town where they might be tortured and killed. It was a strange thought, and he knew it, but he had the eerie feeling that he was hallucinating, that none of this was real.

Lieutenant Rolf Herzog and four troopers took Ben and John to a large house. The lower part was brightly lit, lamps shining through every window. The upper story was dark.

Two men stood guard, but it was plain to John that those inside had already been notified of their arrival.

"What now, Lieutenant Herzog?" John asked.

"Colonel Ward wants to see you. I'll take you inside, under guard, of course."

"Colonel Ward?"

"That's what I said."

John looked at Ben. Ben shrugged, a puzzled look on his face.

The guards removed their handcuffs, but John and Ben marched inside with pistols at their backs. They all waited outside while Herzog went inside. He was gone for about two minutes, then returned.

"Come with me," he said to his prisoners. "You men wait here," he said to the guards. "At attention."

"Yes, sir," one of the men said.

Herzog opened the door and waved Ben and John inside.

They entered a large, spacious room, but one end of it was set off from the rest. On the right, there was a divan, rug, comfortable chairs, bookcases, small tables, such as might be found in any living room owned by a well-to-do family. The other end was more austere, with heavy, dark brown drapes over the windows, a large cherrywood desk, a map table such as draftsmen or cartographers used, a large wall map of the territory, with adjoining states, territories, roads, and topographical features. A man stood behind the desk with colonel's insignia on his shoulderboards. Two other men, a captain and a lieutenant, stood on either side of the desk. The colonel glanced at Ben and John and then down at three separate stacks of papers.

He beckoned to the two men. Ben and John walked toward him, stopped in front of his desk. The colonel looked them both over, but his gaze lingered on John for several seconds, long enough for Savage to feel uncomfortable. John glared at the colonel, who looked to be a tough, hard-bitten man, more accustomed to the saddle than a chair behind a desk.

The other two officers were equally tough looking, with square faces, sun-burnished skin, rock-hard muscles under their uniforms. Their boots were polished to a high sheen. All wore sidearms, flapped black holsters, ammunition pouches on their large belts with shoulder straps.

"Gentlemen," the colonel said, "I regret the inconvenience in detaining you. But some matters of importance have reached my desk, and we are facing a serious situation here. I'm Colonel Lucius Ward, temporary commandant of this post. You are, I believe, John Savage?" Ward stared directly at John, his eyes radiating a steely light.

"I am," John said.

"You bear some resemblance to your father, Dan, especially around the eyes. But you have your mother Clare's nose and mouth, as I remember them."

"You knew my father and mother?"

The colonel did not break his stare.

"Very well, in fact. I'm sorry for your loss, which I only heard about recently." Ward glanced down at one of the stacks of papers, then lifted his gaze back to John. "My son Jesse was also killed at the same time your parents lost their lives."

"You're Jesse's father?" John said, a look of abject surprise on his face.

"Damned if he ain't," Ben said. "Spittin' image, Johnny."

John looked at the colonel more closely. Yes, he could see the strong resemblance. Jesse had been one of those who had joined his father and mother to work the mining claim. He recalled now that Jesse had mentioned that his father was in the military, serving in the army somewhere out West.

"Yes. Jesse was a fine boy. I miss him. Ben, he wrote me seldom, but he always mentioned you and John as good friends. I'm grateful for that."

"Yes, sir, Jesse spoke fondly of you, too, Colonel," Ben said. "But how come you brung us up here at gunpoint? We ain't done nothin'."

"Lieutenant Herzog was not looking for you, Ben, or you, John, but for a man named Oliver Hobart, and one named Armstead Mandrake. A man they call Army, ironically enough."

"Yes, sir, well, we was chasin' the same two men."

"Yes, I'm aware of that now, Ben. From the reports here on my desk, it seems you two have already dispatched some of Hobart's men, those who were responsible for the massacre at Dan's mining camp. Is that correct, John?"

"Colonel, Ben and I were up in a mine when Hobart and his men attacked our camp. We had no weapons. There were a whole lot of them. They shot everybody they saw, including my little sister. Shot them dead. They showed no mercy."

"I did not know your sister. Alice, was it?"

"Yes, sir," John said.

"I'm sorry, son. I share your grief."

"Where is Hobart?" John asked bluntly.

"Ah, we don't know at the moment. But we believe he's somewhere near Fort Laramie. Mandrake, as well. Some other facts have come to my attention. I have patrols out scouring the country, and the village here, searching for those two men and their cohorts."

"How did you get wind of all this?" Ben asked. "Beggin' your pardon, Colonel. We didn't know the army was a-lookin' for them."

"Perhaps you should both sit down, Ben," Ward said. "I can't tell you everything, of course, but some of what I do reveal should send shivers up your spines."

"Hobart hasn't killed somebody up here at the fort, has he?" John said.

"Please sit down, gentlemen. I think you deserve to know some things about Hobart before you continue chasing after him."

"Sir, I won't give up until Hobart and Mandrake are both dead. Either by the gun, or hanging from ropes on the gallows."

Colonel Ward cleared his throat, nodded to Herzog. The lieutenant came up to the desk carrying John's and Ben's pistols. He laid them near the front edge of the desk and stepped back.

John looked at his pistol, still in its holster. He watched as Ward removed it and examined the silver lettering, the scrollwork, with narrowed eyes.

Outside, a horse snorted, and guards called out to one another, marking the hour. It grew quiet in the room as John and Ben settled in the chairs the colonel had indicated.

"Dan made this," Ward said, a pensive tone to his voice, as if he were talking only to himself. "He was a fine craftsman. A fine craftsman."

He set the pistol down next to its holster and came around the desk, sat on one edge.

"I'm afraid, John," Ward said, "that you can no longer take the law into your own hands regarding Hobart and Mandrake. When you hear what I have to say, you will know why."

John said nothing, but he could feel the anger rising in him, seething like a smoldering fire just beneath the surface of his temper, ready to explode and spit fire like a volcano. His mouth was closed tight and air blew through his nostrils as he breathed, clearly audible in the silence of the room.

He sat there, his muscles bunched and coiled as if he were about to spring on the colonel like an enraged tiger and rip out his throat with his bare hands.

21

Colonel Ward turned slightly and waved a
hand over the stacks of documents on his
desk. Then he looked at John Savage, cocking his head, as if wondering how much he
dared confide in the young man.

"There is a great deal at stake here, John,"
Ward said. "I'm chasing a lot more than two
murderers named Mandrake and Hobart.
I've got Cheyenne strayed from the Wind
River country to God knows where. And
somebody has been stealing ordnance from
the armory — rifles, pistols, cartridges. Do
you know what Hobart is up to, why he
headed for Fort Laramie?"

"No, sir, I do not. I only know what he
did in the past."

"You mean . . ."

"I mean, he knew where our mining camp
was, and he rode up there with his men and
just slaughtered every man, woman, and
child he could see."

"He's killed before that," Ward said.

"I'm not surprised."

"But why come here?" Ward asked.

"Do you have any prospectors in those mountains?"

"Why, yes, we do, as a matter of fact." Ward leaned forward, listening attentively, watching John's face.

"Hobart seems to like gold," John said. "He puts a higher price on it than he does human life."

"Granted," Ward said.

"All right. How many men are up there looking for gold, digging it out of the ground, panning it from the creek?"

Ward looked at one of his aides. That man shrugged. He looked at the other one, a second lieutenant.

"Last we counted, there were nearly a hundred miners up on Dead Horse Creek, sir," he said.

"A hundred, then, maybe more now," Ward said. "What are you getting at?"

"Hobart couldn't kill that many men even if those who were with him the day he jumped us were still with him."

"All right."

"So maybe Hobart is behind the theft of all those firearms. And maybe he means to sic those Indians on those miners. How many Indians are missing?"

"About twenty," Ward said. "All young braves, plus a chief, Red Eagle. These are all dangerous men, with many white men's scalps figuratively hanging from their belts."

"Injuns scare hell out of pilgrims," Ben said. "Twenty would be enough for Hobart."

"I'm working in the dark here," Ward said. "All I have are reports and suspicion. No proof. No Hobart. You two were following him, right, John?"

"Yes. Hobart was headed this way."

"You know that for a fact?" Ward asked.

"We do. If this is Fort Laramie, Hobart is already here. Somewhere. And, if I may, Colonel, you have no right to detain us. We've done nothing illegal and we're civilians, not soldiers."

"If I allowed you to roam free, John, you could cause us to lose track of Hobart and never find those escaped Cheyenne, and dozens of lives could be lost."

"Or," John said, "if I promised to let you know where Hobart is hiding and stop him from attacking those miners, you would be in my debt."

"That's surely true," Ward said. "But how can you and Ben here accomplish what this entire post has been unable to do?"

"You don't know what Hobart looks like.

You don't even know what Mandrake looks like. And I have an ace in the hole that you don't even know about."

There was a silence in the room. Outside, the sounds of men's boots echoed on the parade ground, and they could hear the whicker of a horse, the slap of leather, the ring of metal on metal. In another part of the fort, a dog barked, sounding far away and slightly distorted as if the animal was running between buildings.

"What's your ace in the hole, John?" Ward asked.

"Hobart wants to kill me worse than I want to kill him."

"So?"

"So if he knows I'm here and looking for him, he'll come after me. Or he'll send Mandrake to kill me. If we can capture Mandrake, he might talk, tell us where Hobart is."

"Hmmm," Ward intoned. "You have a point there."

"Damned right he has a point," Ben said. "We don't want to be cooped up in the fort, under guard, while that killer Hobart is schemin' to murder more people."

"I will consider it, Ben," Ward said.

John took in a deep breath through his nostrils. He still had some cards to play.

Ward was military, but he was also human. And he had a big stake in Hobart's capture or death. After all, Hobart and his men had murdered his son.

"Colonel," John said, "do you want to know how Jesse died? He was very brave."

"Did you see him . . . were you . . . ?"

"We was watchin' everything, Colonel," Ben said. "We was up in a cave, a-lookin' down at our camp."

"Did Jesse suffer?" Ward asked.

"He tried to save my sister, Alice," John lied. "I mean neither Jesse nor any of the others were armed. Alice screamed when Hobart shot my mother, and Jesse, well, he grabbed her up and tried to protect her with his body."

"That's right," Ben said, picking up on the lie. "He done everything he could to save that girl's life."

"Go on, John," Ward said.

"Hobart himself rode up, rode right up to Alice and Jesse. Shot the both of them. He shot Alice in the head and shot your son in the belly. Jesse still tried to cover Alice when he fell. He didn't know she was dead, I reckon. Hobart let Jesse squirm and suffer before he shot him in the heart."

"That's right. And Hobart liked what he done," Ben said. "He enjoyed makin' poor

Jesse suffer."

Ward bowed his head, squinched his eyes shut to fight back the tears.

"Jesse was brave," John said softly. "Very brave."

A shudder coursed through Colonel Ward's body, but he recovered and straightened up, his back stiff, his eyes narrowed. John thought he could see the flash of hatred in the man's eyes, two burning coals that were emitting sparks through the slits of his lids.

"That sonofabitch," Ward murmured.

"You have to let me try to draw Hobart out in the open, Colonel," John said. "Don't hog-tie me on this. Ben and I rode a long way and we know more about Hobart than you or anyone else on the post."

Ward did not answer right away.

John could see that he was weighing the offer. The other men in the room stood like statues, none daring to venture an opinion.

Ben shot John a look, making a slight nod toward Colonel Ward. John took that to mean that Ben wanted him to push the colonel a little more. At that moment, John was grateful that he had a friend like Ben, a man who would back him up, stand by him through thick and thin, fair weather or foul.

"There's something else, Colonel Ward,"

John said, taking his cue from Ben. "Something you might not know about Ollie Hobart."

"I admit I don't know much about him. He's wanted in a lot of places. He rides, or did ride, with a rough bunch. What else do I need to know, son?"

"Hobart's traveling with a woman. She's as deadly as he is. Her name is Rosa Delgado. Ben and I drove her out of Denver. She owned a saloon there. We've been tracking her and Hobart all this way."

"A woman?" Ward said. He looked around at his aides and at Herzog. They all bore puzzled looks on their faces.

"A Mex woman," Ben said with a quick stab of his voice. "A mighty dangerous gal, that one."

"I did not know this," Ward admitted. "Does it make any difference to you, John? I mean, if she and Hobart were to come after you, meet you face-to-face . . ."

"Do you mean, sir, would I hesitate to shoot a woman?"

"I guess that's what I mean," Ward said, obviously uncomfortable now with a woman in the picture.

"Rosa Delgado picked out her own path. There was a line there, and she stepped over it. Once she took up with Hobart, she called

211

the tune on her own fate. If she faced me with a gun in her hand, I wouldn't even blink an eye. I'd drop the hammer on my pistol once I had her lined up in my sights. To me, she's no different than Hobart now."

"You'd shoot a woman? Kill her, as if she were a man?" Ward said. "That's pretty hard-hearted, John."

"My mother was a woman. My sister might have been. Someone like Rosa Delgado, who picks up a gun and sides with a killer like Hobart, has lost all claim to womanhood. She might as well wear pants and rub away all her rouge. She's not a woman to me anymore. She's a killer, the same as Hobart."

"Hmm. That's interesting, John. I see your point."

"What about letting Ben and me go our own way. We'll stay out of yours, but we don't want to be locked up in a stockade as long as Hobart and his gang are breathing air they stole from my folks, my sister, your son, and all the other men up in that mining camp."

"I don't know," Ward said, still hesitant.

"See that pistol there, Colonel," John said. "My pa made that. He left it to me. It's all I have of him. But there's something else, too, you ought to know."

"What's that?" Ward said.

"Hobart wants that pistol. He sent three men out of Cheyenne to kill me and Ben. Not just because we were dogging his heels, but because he wanted that pistol. And he was willing to pay extra for it."

"You know that for a fact, John?"

"I do. Hobart has got him a worm inside him. It's a worm called Greed. That worm is eating him up. He wants gold, he wants that pistol. He doesn't care a whit about human life. He will kill to get what he wants. You lock me up and that pistol stays out of his reach. If he knows I'm out there, packing iron, he'll want me and the pistol. He'll come after me. He'll make a mistake because that worm is gobbling up his innards."

"Damn, John. You make a good argument. I'm inclined to go along with your logic. It goes against my grain as a soldier. To me, you're taking the law into your own hands and that rankles me, rubs me the wrong way."

"Colonel," John said softly, his voice cutting through the tension in the room, "there wasn't any law when Hobart and his men slaughtered all those innocent people. There wasn't any law around when he was cornered in Rosa's Cantina. He killed one of

213

his own men, just so he could make his escape. I don't claim to be the law, but I want justice, any way I can get it. Don't hog-tie me on this. Let me be to follow the path I chose."

There was a heavy knock on the door, the sound of a commotion outside the room.

"Bradley," Ward barked to the lieutenant standing nearby, "see what the hell's going on."

Lieutenant Winfred Bradley opened the door and a sergeant burst into the room.

"Colonel Ward," he said. "Somebody broke into the armory, killed Sergeant Dixon and Private Means. They carted off rifles and pistols and got clean away."

Sergeant Ray Stoner's words galvanized the officers into action even before Ward issued his orders.

"Sound assembly, Sergeant," he said. "Muster every man jack to the parade ground in ten minutes."

Then he looked at John and Ben.

"Gentlemen, you may strap on your pistols and take your rifles and horses. Leave the post immediately. I don't want to see you or hear about you for at least twenty-four hours. That clear?"

John and Ben both shot from their chairs as if they were propelled by an unseen force.

In seconds, they had strapped on their pistols. They pushed their way past soldiers coming and going.

"You take care, Savage," Herzog said. "You get in our way and Colonel Ward won't hesitate to blow you both to kingdom come."

"Herzog," John said. "You got a big chunk in your craw. You stay out of my way, or the same goes for you."

Ben and John stepped out into the night. Their horses stood there at the hitchrail. The two troopers stepped aside as John and Ben mounted. No one challenged them as they rode across the parade ground, which was filling with men at arms. The brassy sound of a bugle calling them to muster filled the air with curdling notes that sounded as feral, foreboding, and chilling as the howl of a timber wolf on the prowl.

Hobart's head bobbed up as if jerked by an invisible cord. He cocked it to one side, listening to the sound of pounding hoofbeats.

Army Mandrake strode to the front window of the house. He slid the heavy curtain aside and peered out into the starlit darkness.

"Uh-oh," he said.

"Who is it?" Hobart asked, rising to his feet. He pushed away from the table where he had been studying a crudely drawn map. His right hand dropped to his side. His fingers closed around the butt of his pistol.

The hoofbeats grew louder.

"It looks like Captain Fry."

"Alone?"

"Yep. Wearin' out leather. This ain't goin' to be good, Ollie."

"He's got some explaining to do," Hobart said. "Let him in."

The hoofbeats stopped as Captain Jubal Fry hauled his horse to a stop at the hitchrail outside the house. He sprang from his horse, hit the ground running. He left the reins dangling, knowing the horse would stay right where he stopped. His boots sounded thuds and squeaks on the pine porch as Army opened the door.

"Army, we got big trouble," Fry said as he entered the room. His eyes went wide as he saw Ollie standing there behind the table, ready to draw his pistol.

Fry's uniform was wrinkled, the armpits black with sweat. He was a hollow-cheeked man, gaunt, spindly-legged, with short, black sideburns, a thin moustache, close-cropped dark hair greased to a high shine. His kerchief hung loose around his neck, its insides dark with sweat and grime.

"You-you Oliver Hobart?" Fry asked when he had recovered from his surprise.

"I'm Hobart, Captain Fry. Let's hear about this trouble. Make it quick and short. You were supposed to deliver another shipment of rifles and ammunition to Army yesterday."

"Aw, Ollie, Jubal's okay. He can't always sneak rifles off the post."

"He can talk, can't he?" Ollie said, his impatience showing in a muscle that rippled along his left jawline.

Rosa Delgado sat in a chair that was in shadow at one corner of the room. She had a half-filled bottle of whiskey next to her, on the floor. She picked it up and held it out toward Fry.

"Have a drink, soldier," she said, her words slurred as if her tongue had been bee-stung and swelled up.

Fry looked at Rosa, nonplussed. He was military, stood as straight and stiff as if he had an iron rod for a backbone. He didn't acknowledge the drunken offer, but turned his gaze back to Ollie.

"Yes, I can talk, Hobart. I rode out of a damned hornet's nest tonight over at the post. All hell's done broke loose. Army, I thought you had them Injuns under control."

"What in hell are you talkin' about, Jubal?" Army said.

"Stay out of this, Army," Ollie said. "I'll ask the questions. Captain, why don't you sit down and talk some sense. You want some whiskey?"

"No," Fry said. "No whiskey." He walked to the table, pulled out a chair, sat down. He sat as stiff as when he was standing up. That ramrod for a backbone, Ollie figured. Ollie sat down, too, and nodded for Army to take a seat.

"First I knew something was wrong," Fry said, "was when Chet Newgate, Lieutenant Newgate, he's the quartermaster, come running into my office sayin' a bunch of redskins had broke into the armory and was haulin' out rifles and cartridges. I thought maybe it was Red Eagle, but no, these was Injuns I never seen before. They didn't make no noise and they had pack-horses lined up like they was at mornin' muster. The two men guardin' the ordnance was lyin' dead, their throats cut from ear to ear."

Ollie looked at Mandrake.

"You know anything about this, Army?"

Mandrake shook his head.

"Somethin's damned sure wrong, Ollie. But, Jubal, you was supposed to bring us them rifles two days ago."

"I couldn't pull it off, Army. Colonel Ward's in a high dither over reports about them Injuns up on the Wind River breakin' out and some other stuff."

"What other stuff?" Ollie asked, spearing Fry with a daggered look.

"Colonel Ward's son was killed at a mining camp down in Colorado a while back. He got wind that the leader of the gang was headed this way. He's been sending out patrols to hunt this jasper down."

Ollie sucked in a breath.

"You know the name of this gang leader, Captain?" Ollie asked, exhaling.

Fry shook his head.

"Nope. But I think the colonel knows. He's keeping everything he knows real tight. No names. Well, most names."

"What's that mean?" Ollie asked. "What names have you heard?"

"I don't know who they are, but one of the privates mentioned that a patrol he was on had also been looking for two men that might be heading for Fort Laramie."

"Names?" Ollie's irritation showed on his florid face, on the muscle that twitched along his jawline, and on the swelling veins in his neck.

"A young feller name of John something. And a man named Russell. Ben Russell, I think."

Ollie stiffened in his chair as if he'd had an icicle dropped down inside the back of his shirt. His eyes flickered, then narrowed to rattlesnake slits.

"John Savage," he said, his voice a breathy loud whisper. "Was the last name Savage?"

Fry's expression did not change. Instead, his eyes turned agate hard and shone as if a lamp had been lit behind them.

"Yes. Savage was the name. John Savage."

"Oh shit," Mandrake said.

Ollie glared at Army. Rosa gave out a small cry. It sounded like the squeal of a puppy that had been kicked.

"I do not think you will get the *pistola* from John Savage," Rosa slurred. "Not in the way you expect, Ollie."

"You shut up, Rosa," Ollie said.

"You do not want to hear the truth, Ollie."

Ollie turned his head to look at her, his eyes boring into hers with a fierce, withering stare. Rosa lifted the bottle and took another sip of whiskey. Her eyes grew cloudy and dull. She closed them as the whiskey seeped down her throat and ignited her veins.

"How the hell could a bunch of redskins sneak into the armory and steal rifles and cartridges?" Ollie asked, fixing Fry with a look that was almost unchanged from the one he had given Rosa.

"All I can figure is they had help and they knew which throats to slit. Hell, they didn't make a damned sound. Ain't no walls around Laramie."

"Injuns, that many of 'em, ain't invisible," Ollie said.

"These sure as hell were."

"Where in hell was Major Cresswell?" Army asked. "Wasn't he helpin' you, Jubal?"

Fry's shoulders lifted in a shrug, sank back to normal.

"George was supposed to meet me two days ago and let me know when I could have the rifles to bring you."

"And?" Ollie said.

"He didn't come by, so I went to see him. He said there was a snag."

"A snag?"

"That's what he said. 'Tomorrow,' he said, and yesterday he brushed me back again, like he was swatting a damned fly."

"What do you make of that, Captain?" Ollie asked.

Fry raised his head, stroked the bottom of his chin as if testing the closeness of his shave, or trying to collect his thoughts. Ollie waited. So did Army.

"I think he sold us out, Hobart." There was no quaver in Fry's voice. He laid his hands flat on the table as if he had just spread out the winning hand in a poker game. "I think he threw in with the Cheyenne and plumb sold us out."

"Why in hell would he do that?" Hobart asked. "And where did a bunch of renegade redskins get the money?"

"And why in hell didn't you come to me

yesterday and tell me about this?" Army asked.

"Hey, back off, Army. You, too, Hobart. I ain't the enemy here. You made the deal with Major Cresswell. You dangled the pork in front of him. Not me."

"He sure as hell took the money," Army said. "Agreed to the deal. Licked his lips when I put greenbacks in his hand. I figured him for a greedy bastard."

"You know anything about Major George Cresswell, Army? I mean, where he comes from, who he really is?"

"He's just another soldier to me," Army said. "Why?"

"Yeah," Ollie said, leaning forward over the table, his eyes almost feral in their intensity. Fry straightened his back and pulled his head back as if he were at attention, but he was really bracing himself for a blow from those big fists of Ollie Hobart.

"Cresswell, when he was a boy, I mean a little boy, maybe four or five, was in a wagon train heading out West from St. Louis. I think his folks were going out to Oregon or maybe Santa Fe. Anyways, the wagon train got hit by a bunch of Sioux and Cheyenne. His folks were killed and the Sioux took him prisoner. Raised him. Raised him like a damned Injun."

"A Sioux," Ollie said. "Those Injuns we're dealin' with are Cheyenne, ain't they, Army?"

"Far as I know," Army said.

"George was sold to the Cheyenne, the Northern Cheyenne, the way he tells it, when he was about sixteen or so. He grew up speakin' Sioux and Cheyenne, knows the sign lingo. Couple years later, he was in some Injun camp when the soldiers came up and shot it to pieces. Cresswell was taken and remembered enough English so the soldiers didn't kill him right then."

Army leaned forward, caught up in the story.

"Then what happened?" Mandrake said.

"George was adopted by Colonel Roland Cresswell, sent off to school back East, joined the army, and, because he was a good fighter, and smart, he kept getting promoted. Far as I know, he never fought Sioux nor Cheyenne before. He was chasin' Apaches down south with Crook and Miles. He come up here six months ago."

Ollie leaned back in his chair, his forehead wrinkling in thought.

Army looked at him, his mouth agape.

Fry's breathing was the only sound in the room for a long moment. He sat there, stiff as a board, his expression noncommittal as the homeliest desert stone.

"Army," Ollie said, "we can't wait no more. We get Red Eagle and his bunch and we hit them miners up in Dead Horse Canyon."

"When?" Mandrake said.

"We'll ride up tomorrow night. We got enough guns. Make sure them Injuns carry their war clubs. Hell, we'll use slingshots if we have to. There's gold up there aplenty and it hasn't gone down to no assay office."

"Tomorrow night? It's a day's ride," Army said.

"We'll hit 'em when they wake up, the day after."

"If you say so," Army said. "I hope Red Eagle's still up there in his mountain camp."

"He'd better be," Ollie said.

"What about Cresswell?" Fry said. "He might beat you to Red Eagle."

"You know why he's gone Injun on us, Fry?" Ollie asked.

Fry let out a breath, looked down at his hands, then back up at Hobart.

"There's been talk of a campaign up north to round up all the Sioux and Cheyenne and either put 'em on a reservation or kill 'em. Folks are going into the Black Hills, findin' gold, and the Sioux are hoppin' mad. I think Cresswell's going to help his red

225

brothers by takin' rifles and cartridges up to the Dakotas and joinin' in the fight."

"On the wrong side," Hobart said.

"Yeah. On the wrong side."

Hobart stood up, a look of distaste on his face.

"You know what, Army?" he said.

"What, Ollie?"

"I think we just stepped into a deep pile of shit."

There wasn't a bit of humor in Ollie's words. He walked back to where Rosa was sitting, jerked the whiskey bottle out of her hand, and slapped her hard across the mouth.

"And I'm just about to run out of patience with you, too, Rosa. Make some coffee and drink it down until you sober up."

"Ollie," she said in a pleading voice that trailed off with her sodden breath.

"If you don't," he said, "you'll be the first blood I draw on this job. Long before we hit that mining camp."

For the first time that evening, Fry lost his composure. He slumped in his chair, his military bearing gone like a puff of smoke.

But he never said a word.

23

John swung into the saddle, relieved to be free of Colonel Ward's jurisdiction. He would have been less relieved had he heard what the colonel said to Lieutenant Herzog as soon as Ben and John walked out the door.

"Rolf, get two good men and follow Savage and Russell. Don't be obvious about it. Keep your distance. But I want to know where they go and what they do."

"Yes, sir," Herzog said. "Do you want me to detain them if they come across Hobart?"

"No, just send one of your men back here to report."

Herzog saluted and left to get two troopers so that he could follow John and Ben. He wasted no time, but outside, he marked the direction the two riders were headed and ran to his horse, calling out to his men: "Crisp, Freeman, come with me. The rest of you are dismissed."

The two sergeants, Will Crisp and Daryl Freeman, flanked him on their horses a few minutes later. Herzog gave them their orders and the three men slowly rode into the night, following in the tracks of their quarry, stopping every so often to listen, making sure they were following the two civilians.

Ben growled at John.

"You mind tellin' me where in hell we're goin', Johnny?"

John was leaning to one side, peering down at the ground.

"Wherever these tracks lead us."

"What tracks?"

"See them all? You heard what happened? Some Indians broke into the armory and stole rifles and cartridges. Probably for Hobart. If we follow their tracks, we might find Ollie."

Ben leaned over and scanned the ground. Scanned the blackness, struggling to find even the faintest trace of a hoofprint, an iron scuff mark, a broken twig, or anything besides ground as black as funeral crepe.

"I don't see no tracks," Ben said.

"At night, you have to compare."

"Compare what?"

"Bare ground with torn-up ground."

"All looks the same to me."

"Pa taught me to track at night. Black night, when there wasn't any moon and the stars were faint."

Ben tilted his head back, looked up at the sky. There were stars sprinkled everywhere, tiny pieces of shattered, broken glass shot with light. A glow in the sky from a moon not yet risen. He looked back down at the ground. But he didn't trust his eyes. At night, all shapes were suspicious, unreal. He might have seen horse tracks. He might be just imagining them. He didn't know.

"I can't compare shit," Ben said.

"There's that, too," John said.

"Huh?"

"Smell the horse droppings? They're faint, but they're down there, and I can see them, too."

"Maybe you better explain how you see anything down there on that black ground."

"I don't see much, but if I shift my focus, I can make out tracks. I look up and down and right and left. The faint light makes tracks appear kind of not direct, but indirect. Hard to explain."

"Let it go, Johnny," Ben said. "I ain't even goin' to try and understand you. Life is just too short."

John laughed.

He could smell the horse droppings and the ground was roiled enough so that he knew there had been horses along their path not long before. The riders seemed to be heading for the distant mountains, mountains he could not see in the darkness of night. But with his vision, he already knew that some of the horses were carrying more weight than others. All of the hoofprints seemed deeply embedded in the sandy soil. If packhorses were carrying rifles and ammunition, their tracks would be the most visible. All of the horses were unshod, so the tracks were not as distinct had the horses been wearing shoes. However, one track stood out. And that one had been made from a shod horse.

"Something funny here, Ben," John said, pulling on his reins to halt his horse.

"Yeah? What?"

"Can you see well enough to make out that the bunch of horses has been splitting up? Some go one way, others drift off in another direction. I'm going to follow just one set of tracks."

"I can't see much. Ground looks torn up some, but . . ."

"No matter. I think whoever's ridin' these horses will meet up later. I think they're trying to throw off any army trackers."

"Makes sense," Ben said.

The moon rose above the horizon, slipped up slow, half lit, the shining half beaming with an alabaster radiance that seemed to pulse with a quiet energy that John could feel. The landscape changed under its light. Shadows formed and reformed, plants that had been nearly invisible before now blossomed on the plain, taking on grotesque shapes that made them seem alive and oddly ominous. The effect, John thought, was spectral, as if the ghosts of living things had magically appeared and what had been flat and dark before now bristled with a life born of the night, born out of nothingness.

"We gonna just wait here and gaze at the moon?" Ben asked quietly when John had not spoken for several minutes.

"Awhile, yes."

"How come?"

"Adjust the eyes, for one thing."

"All right. Any other reason? We can see a little better. I mean I can see some horse tracks now."

John swung out of the saddle, walked over to a pile of horse apples. Another horse had stepped in it and dragged some of the nuggets away from the pile, cracked some of them open. John knelt down and sniffed the offal. Ben eyed him from atop his horse, feeling oddly out of place, almost unwelcome and unwanted.

"Not so fresh," John said. "But not real old, either. A couple of hours ahead of us, maybe."

"I'm thinkin' maybe we don't want to catch up to them thievin' Injuns whilst it's still dark as a mine shaft out here."

John looked back over the way they had come, turned his head slowly, cocked it, cupped one ear with his hand. He held up another to silence Ben as he listened. He turned his head slightly to the right and to the left. He still cupped an ear, bending the flesh slightly. Gathering sound in a human seashell. Amplifying whatever he thought he had heard moments before. Listening, like a deer, for anything that made a sound.

John heard something.

He drew in a breath, took his hand away from his ear. He turned to look up at Ben and put a finger to his lips.

Ben nodded.

John beckoned to him. Ben dismounted, led his horse over. He stood next to John, a puzzled expression on his face. He said nothing, knowing he was still under John's admonition to keep silent.

"Ben, we might have a small hitch here. Just listen to me." John's whisper was just loud enough for Ben to hear without straining. He nodded again.

"I think somebody's following us," John said. "Maybe Colonel Ward sicced some soldiers on our tail. Or those Indians we're tracking might have circled around, some of them, anyway, and mean to catch us from behind."

John paused and Ben nodded again.

"Either way, we have to take it into account. I was going to follow the tracks of that one shod horse. If that's a stolen army horse, we can deal with that. But if there's a soldier leading those Indians, he'd be the one who might be in cahoots with Ollie Hobart. Follow my thinking so far?"

"Yeah," Ben said, without thinking.

"I don't much like this bunch splitting up like they have. Those we don't follow might circle in back of us. In fact, that's what I would do if I was leading these Indians."

"I follow you," Ben whispered.

"We can't split up. They could pick us off too easy."

"I agree," Ben said.

"We can do two things, the way I see it. We can keep following that shod horse and the two Indians with it. I'm pretty sure those two other sets of tracks are carrying Indians, not rifles. The hoof marks are not deep enough. So those three men are more dangerous. They're not protecting their stolen goods. They can ride away from us if we catch up to them. Or they can swarm over us and shoot us dead if each one comes at us from a different direction."

"You're scarin' the hell out of me, Johnny."

"I know. I'm scared, too. Just working all this out in my mind."

"Well, go on then. What are we goin' to do?"

"The Indians and the man on the shod horse, who might be a soldier, are about two hours ahead of us. So we can track them for nearly two hours, if they don't ride on solid rock. Gives us time to maybe find out who's behind us."

"How do you expect to do that?" Ben asked.

"I don't know if those boys behind us are trackers, but I expect they are."

"So?"

"My idea is to ride for another hour and a half, then drop off my horse at a good spot and lie in wait. You'd take Gent and go on, leaving our two sets of tracks."

"I don't much like that idea. You don't know how many men are maybe following us and they might shoot you dead."

"If they wanted to kill us, they would

already have jumped us, Ben."

Ben sighed.

"You got a point, John. So you wait for them. You see them. Then what?"

"If they're soldiers, sent after us just to see where we go, I'll make them an offer."

"Yeah? What offer?"

"I'll ask them to join us."

"What?"

"Why not? Colonel Ward wants his rifles back. And he wants Hobart. We both have the same aim, don't you think?"

"I think you're speculatin' a mite too much, Johnny."

"I might be at that."

"But your daddy used to say, 'a plan is better'n no plan at all.'"

"He did say that. So what do you think? You like my idea?"

"Not much," Ben said.

"Good, that's what we'll do then."

John grinned. Ben gave him a sour look. The moon bathed their faces in an eerie light. Their eyes were hollow pits. Shadows took weight and years from Ben's face, hollowed John's visage to a gaunt and ghostly image. They stood there in the silence for several seconds.

"Mount up, Ben. Let's follow these tracks."

Both men climbed back into their saddles.

John led the way, following three sets of horse tracks. One set was shod, the others, smaller and unshod. Indian ponies. The horses were walking, not running, and when John looked off in the distance, the mountains were closer, dark hulks that loomed under snowcapped peaks that stood like dim beacons in the sky, nearly as bright as the moon.

They rode for an hour. John kept his bearings, wondering if the tracks would veer, start making a circle to join up with the others. But in that hour the tracks headed straight for the mountains. And the mountains grew larger and darker. Clouds drifted over the moon, floated above them, shifting the light, making his task more difficult each time it happened.

Ben and John chewed on jerky and hardtack and drank water from their canteens. Not at the same time, but at alternate intervals. This was John's idea and Ben agreed. One of them had to be ready to shoot or sound an alarm. They were not gaining ground on their quarry, but holding their own, staying two hours behind.

A few minutes later, John drew in hard on his reins. Gent stopped. Ben pulled up alongside him and stopped his horse. He had been nodding in the saddle, trying to stay awake.

"Yeah? How come you're stopping?" Ben asked.

John pointed to the ground.

Ben leaned over, looked where John was pointing.

"I don't see nothin'," Ben said.

"No. Neither do I."

"What do you mean, Johnny?"

"I mean, no more tracks."

Both men stared down at bare, unmarked ground. The horse tracks had vanished, suddenly, it seemed. They both straightened up and looked all around. The moon stood high overhead, shining bright as polished marble. The land lay in shadow, not a tall silhouette to be seen.

It seemed to John as if the world had gone dead. There wasn't a sound. There was no movement. The earth stood still, empty, barren of all life save their own. Ben shivered involuntarily.

John closed his eyes for a moment, then opened them, to make sure he wasn't dreaming.

He knew, then, they had been tricked. They were not standing on bare rock. But there were no more tracks.

Where had the riders gone? Turned into

phantoms? Plucked from the earth by some mysterious force or being?

For a moment, he wondered if he had been addled by the moonlight. He had heard of such things as a boy. Lunacy, wasn't that what they called it? He looked up at the moon and wondered. Its half face seemed as enigmatic as the earth had become. Not a trace of life above or below.

Only the two of them, he and Ben, lost, alone, and probably in danger the longer they stayed there. He lowered his head and stared back down at the ground.

He wasn't crazy, he knew. There had to be an explanation for the vanishing tracks.

And, for sure, the change was ominous. Ominous as hell.

24

John handed the reins of his horse to Ben.

"Hold these. Wait here. I'll be back."

John walked over their backtrail, hunching over to study the ground. When he came upon the place where the tracks appeared again, he began walking in circles, still backtracking. It was difficult to see and he was careful not to step in any of the horse tracks.

Finally, he stopped, knelt down and saw what he had been looking for.

Moccasin tracks.

He followed these, again avoiding any obliteration of these with his own boots.

Ben lost sight of John in the darkness after he walked away. He felt very alone out there. Gent pawed the ground, blew air through his nostrils. His own horse stood hipshot, head drooping. There was no grass there for either horse.

He could hear John's footsteps, and then

even those faded away into the deepening silence.

He listened to his own breathing, became aware of the beating of his heart. Like most men, Ben was not used to being alone in a strange place. It felt almost unnatural to him. With the faint throb of his heart, he felt mortal, exposed. He thought of all the people Hobart had killed and of all the men he and John had killed, and realized how brief life could be. He could go in the next second. A rifle shot out of nowhere, an Indian leaping onto his back, squeezing his neck, shutting off the breath. It could be that quick. His life could be that short.

He began to sweat and his palms turned clammy in the chill that seeped down from the mountains. His throat constricted with a sudden dryness and his breathing became more audible, so loud he was sure the sound would carry for miles and . . .

"You awake, Ben?" John said.

Ben's backbone creaked as his head snapped up. A rush of fear shot through his veins.

"John, you nigh scared me to death. You oughtn't to sneak up on a man like that."

"I didn't sneak up. I think you were dozing, Ben."

"I warn't dozin'. I just didn't hear you."

"I found out what the Indians did. One Indian, anyway."

John took the reins from Ben and climbed back into the saddle.

"You gonna tell me, or just keep it to yourself?" Ben asked.

"Pretty smart what they did," John said. "Gathered a bunch of sage, pulled them up out of the ground, wove them all together and made a big old broom."

"A broom?"

"Kind of like a broom. They've been brushing away their tracks, sweeping them clean."

Ben tilted his hat back on his head and scratched along his hairline.

"Yeah. Pretty damned smart," he said.

"That two hours lead they had on us has shrunk some. Hell, they could be waiting for us most anywhere."

"And we can't foller 'em no more."

"Not in this dark. Even I can't see those sagebrush marks sitting on top of Gent here. I'd have to crawl along on my hands and knees. It's not worth it."

"No," Ben said. "So now what?"

"So now, we ride off a ways and wait."

"Wait for what?"

"I put my ear to the ground back there and heard hoofbeats. Pretty faint. But whoever's following us is moving right along. I listened for quite a while, seems like. Soldiers, I figure. Walk a ways, trot some, then a gallop, and back to a walk."

"How close?" Ben asked.

John turned his horse, beckoned to Ben.

"Close enough that I can feel soldiers breathing down my neck."

Ben clapped spurs to his horse's flanks and followed John.

"We gonna hide, John?" Ben asked as he caught up to Savage.

"No place to hide. We'll just wait and see if we can't get the drop on them. Better shake out your rifle. But don't shoot. I just want them to see we mean business."

John pulled his rifle from its scabbard. He reined in Gent a few moments later and slid out of the saddle. Ben did the same. They stood there in the darkness, listening, waiting, watching their backtrail for as far as they could see.

"I ain't got a cartridge in the chamber," Ben said.

"Leave it be, Ben. We're not going to shoot anybody."

"We ain't? Then, why the rifles?"

"We'll use them as persuaders. Now keep quiet."

Ben opened his mouth to say something

else, but closed it again. He laid the barrel of his rifle across his pommel and looked up at the stars, the frozen moon half in shadow. The distant cry of a timber wolf floated down from the foothills, hung in the air like a solitary scream from hell, then vanished into silence.

The scent of sage, musty and cloying, flared in John's nostrils as he sat his horse, listening, sparing his eyes from light by keeping his gaze on the darkest shadows sprawling across the landscape. He knew that when he needed to see those soldiers who were following them, he could make them out long before they saw him.

It was not a long wait.

John heard the scuffle of shod hooves, the swishing rustle of sagebrush and sand a few moments before the three riders came into view. All three of them were gazing at the ground, leaning out of their saddles like gawkers staring into a tidepool in some dark, dismal swamp. He repressed the urge to chuckle.

Three blind men following a cold trail, he thought.

"Now, Ben," John whispered. "Follow me."

John kicked Gent into action. The horse's muscles bunched up and flowed into rippling energy, propelling its large body forward toward the three uniformed soldiers.

"Hold up there," John said, his voice deep with authority. He held his rifle straight up, pointing at the sky, the butt anchored to his calf.

"Whoa," Herzog said to his horse. "Hold up," he said to his men.

The three horses stopped as Ben and John rode up.

"Savage? That you?"

"We mean you no harm, Lieutenant," John said. "Hear me out."

He looked at the two men riding with Herzog, saw their sergeant's stripes, their rugged faces blank with surprise.

"You throwing down on me. Two against three."

"You're following me, aren't you, Herzog?"

"That's Lieutenant Herzog. Maybe I am. Maybe I'm not."

"Well, why strain your eyes, Lieutenant? Ben and I are following a shod horse and two Indian ponies. Only their tracks petered out. I thought you and your sergeants might want to ride along with us. Save you trying to track us. You can be stubborn about it, or you can take me up on my offer."

Herzog did not answer right away. John could see that he was mulling the offer over in his military mind.

"Why are you tracking these men?" Herzog asked. "This is army business."

"You mean stolen rifles," John said.

"That's right."

"Well, the rifles are headed northwest. The main body of Indians broke off a ways back and headed that way. Reason I'm following these particular tracks is one of the horses is shod. The others aren't. I figure there's a white man behind this, and he's going to lead me to Ollie Hobart."

"That what you figure?" Herzog asked.

"That's what I said. If you want your rifles back, you're on the wrong trail, Lieutenant."

"We can't take on fifteen or twenty Indians."

"Then, why not go with us? There'd be five of us against three. The tracks have been brushed out, but I reckon the white man and the two redskins with him are heading straight for those mountains yonder."

John cocked a thumb toward the black humps behind him.

"I don't know. It would be highly irregular," Herzog said.

John looked at the two sergeants. Their

expressions were noncommittal. They stared back, impassive as store-window dummies.

"What's irregular is you and your men following Ben and me. We had nothing to do with the theft of those rifles. We're not the enemy. But if my hunch is right, Hobart's behind this. He wants to use the Cheyenne to rob those miners somewhere up in those mountains."

"I know where the prospectors are," Herzog said. "But there's probably a camp of renegade Indians not far from there. If your hunch is right, Cresswell could be headed that way."

"Cresswell?"

"Major George Cresswell. He was in command of the armory. We believe he's in cahoots with the Cheyenne who left the reservation up on the Wind River. He was captured as a kid, raised by Ogallala Sioux. He's even got an Indian name. They call him Tashunka Gleska. Spotted Horse. Army figured he would be a big help fighting Indians. Now Colonel Ward thinks he's helping the Cheyenne. For some reason we don't know."

"Cresswell know Hobart?" John asked.

"Could be. Hobart, we think, is behind the earlier thefts of ordnance and maybe lured some twenty or so Cheyenne away from Wind River."

"Well, you're never going to find out if you stop me and Ben from going after Cresswell."

"My orders were not to stop you from anything, Savage."

"Look, Lieutenant, why don't you call me John and I'll call you, what's your first name, anyway?"

"Rolf."

"That okay with you, Rolf?"

Herzog sucked in a breath through his nostrils. One of the sergeants, Daryl Freeman, screwed his face up in an expression of distaste.

"All right, John. Say we go with you after Cresswell. There are no tracks, you say. How do you figure to track him?"

"I think those Indians will get tired of sweeping up after their ponies and drop the sagebrush broom. We'll find more tracks by morning. And once they get into the mountains, they'll leave sign that can't be brushed away."

"You a tracker, John?"

"I can read a broken branch, a turned-over stone, an iron scuff mark on a flat rock."

"You're a tracker," Herzog said.

As they rode off toward the mountains,

247

Herzog introduced his two sergeants, Daryl Freeman and Will Crisp, to Ben and John. After that, all five men were on a first-name basis.

"How far ahead do you figure Cresswell is, John?" Herzog asked.

"Probably an hour or so. He's not in any hurry. Maybe less than that. Just be ready in case any of those three double back on us."

After that, none of the men spoke. John followed the brush marks, when he could see them, and they were as good as horse tracks.

When they got to the foothills, John reined up, halting the entire party. He pointed to the ground.

"There are the tracks," he said. "Any idea where Cresswell might be headed, Rolf?"

Herzog stared ahead at the looming mountains.

"I think so," he said. "Hard to tell, it's so dark, but I recognize these hills. If the tracks veer off to the left, I'd say Cresswell and the two Cheyenne are headed up Dead Horse Canyon."

"Dead Horse Canyon?" John asked.

"That's where the prospectors are. And probably where Hobart and the Cheyenne have their camp."

The sky began to pale when they found the entrance to Dead Horse Canyon. The morning star hung like a sparkling diamond in the sky. The moon was losing its glow. In the east, dawn was beginning to flow in a creamy line just above the horizon. An owl floated from the pine trees and flapped on silent wings to a higher perch somewhere up the dark and forbidding defile of Dead Horse Canyon.

There was not a sound to be heard when the five men stopped to listen just inside the canyon.

The tracks they had been following were no longer heading in that direction. John pointed to the ground, showed Herzog that the tracks were leading off into the pines toward a ridge to the north.

"Be suicide to ride up this canyon," John said.

"I agree." Herzog patted his horse's neck. "We'll have to flank them."

"We'll make a lot of noise, Rolf. They'll hear us for sure," John said.

"Any ideas, then?" Herzog asked.

John looked at the ridge to the left of the canyon. It rose like the backbone of a prehistoric beast, its top bristling with pine trees that offered concealment and muffling of sound.

"How far up are those prospectors, Rolf?"

"About three or four miles. Canyon widens a little ways ahead."

"Follow me," John said, and turned Gent into the trees at the foot of the ridge to their left. Four men followed John, none of them knowing of his plan, but trusting him. There was a bond between them now that had not existed before. Not one of them questioned his leadership.

Somehow, they all sensed that John Savage had a plan, even though none knew what it was.

A rising sun painted the dawn sky, daubing it a crimson the color of maple leaves in the fall, brilliant and raging with a sailor's warning. The morning star disappeared and the moon turned into an empty shell being scrubbed away by an invisible hand.

Daylight came slow on the ridge and in the bosom of the mountains. And so, too, did the fear of what lay ahead beyond the bloodred horizon.

25

George Cresswell held up his hand, signaling a halt to the two Ogallala riding behind him. He pointed to the flat rock just to his right. The stone jutted from the earth like a ledge. He had been to this place before, and underneath the ledge were dead limbs, sticks of wood, a tin box full of shavings, a flat piece of iron, and another piece shaped like a small horseshoe.

He signed to the two redmen with him, one a Lakota of the Hunkpapa tribe, the other a Northern Cheyenne. All three men dismounted, then tied their horses to juniper bushes. The Lakota was called Talking Hawk; the Cheyenne had the name of Broken Thumb. Both wore buckskins, moccasins, beaded loin cloths.

Cresswell dug into his saddlebag and pulled out a clay pipe with a long wooden stem carved from a willow tree. The bowl of the pipe was square, its pale pink exterior polished smooth. Then he pulled forth a pouch of tobacco.

He pointed to the flint and steel beneath the rock, the wood and shavings. Thumb and Talking Hawk squatted down and lifted the items up to the rock shelf, then started to make a fire. Cresswell sat down on the edge and took off his cavalry boots and spurs. He stood up and removed his tunic, cap, pistol belt, and trousers. Hawk walked to his horse and removed a bundle from his saddlebags. He carried the bundle to Cresswell and handed it to him.

Cresswell untied the leather thongs that bound the bundle, unfolded a fringed buckskin shirt, beaded moccasins, trousers, and leggings. He donned the clothes while the small fire blazed. Thumb added more sticks to it.

Cresswell filled the pipe, removed a flaming faggot from the fire, lit the tobacco. He squatted on one side of the fire and bade his two companions to sit. He puffed on the pipe. Then he took a generous pinch of tobacco from the pouch and tossed some into the fire at the four directions. He handed the pipe to Hawk.

"I am now Tashunka Gleska," Cresswell said, speaking in Lakota and signing with his hands. "I am no longer a white face. I am Ogallala as long as grass grows and water flows from the Paha Sapa."

"That is good," Hawk said. "You are Lakota. You are Spotted Horse."

Thumb grunted and spoke in the Cheyenne tongue, his hands like birds, making the sign. "Spotted Horse is a redman. He is no longer a white face. He is brave. He is good."

"Hear my words, Wakan Tanka," Cresswell said. "Give me strength to fight my enemies. Make me strong and let me return to my people."

The three men passed the pipe until the tobacco was smoked, each saying words to the Great Spirit, Wakan Tanka.

Cresswell held the smoke in his lungs until it began to burn, then let it slowly flow from his nostrils. He watched the smoke hang in the air for a moment, then slowly dissipate. Battens of fog clung to the sides of the ridge and he watched wisps of it detach and float like smoke. Tendrils rose from the rocks and into the air, as if the smoke headed toward heaven.

He felt free for the first time in a long while. His conscience was at ease. He had been no less a prisoner of the white man than he had been with the red. But over the years, he had seen what his fellow white men had done to the Lakota, the Cheyenne, the Crow, and the Blackfeet. Treaties broken, promises forgotten, good, strong men driven like cattle to places they didn't want to go.

Some of the men he had grown up with in the Dakotas had been reduced to beggars and outcasts, scorned and cursed by soldiers, whiskey peddlers, land grabbers, and prospectors. The injustice of it all had been eating away at him for a long time. Now, he had broken free of the white man's grip and could return to a simpler life, a life where the people had respect for the land and believed in a Great Spirit and the spirit that was in all things. The redman knew things the white man never considered in his headlong rush to acquire land, gold, and the subjugation of a proud and noble people.

The air in the mountains was sweet, and the smoke represented the spirit, the breath made visible, the soul that was free to roam the skies and the land. His chest and the chests of his two companions bore the scars of the Sun Dance and that gave him comfort now that he was not encased in a military uniform. He took no pride in being a white man. Not anymore. His skin was white, but his soul was as red as the iron-rich earth.

He had long ago given up his hatred for the Lakota who had killed his parents. He understood their reasons. The white man had invaded the redman's birthplace, the land given to him by the Great Spirit, Wakan Tanka. The redman was not the enemy. He had known this for a long time and yet his military training had held him captive. But when he saw the Cheyenne and the Lakota, the other tribes of the plains, sent to reservations, kept there like animals in a zoo, his heart had rebelled, his conscience had begun to hurt as if it had been pricked by a thorn that dug deeper and deeper until he carried a festering wound that none could see.

Hobart had proven to be the last straw. He was another white man, a murderous, greedy white man, who wanted to use the Cheyenne to attack prospectors, steal their gold, risk their lives for a few moments of freedom. It was wrong. All of it was wrong, and he was now filled with a hatred for all white faces, and especially for Hobart, Mandrake, Tanner, Fry, and all the others who would exploit the redman and further degrade the character of a proud and noble race who only wanted to live in harmony with the earth and the sky. It galled him to think these thoughts and now, in his mind, he placed them in the bowl of the pipe, and released them in the smoke that rose to the sky and became part of all things, like spirit.

They finished the ceremonial smoke and Cresswell put the pipe and tobacco back in his saddlebag.

"Now," he said, "we go to our brothers and tell them to come with us to the north."

"Yes," Thumb said.

Hawk said yes, too.

The sun was a boiling disk on the eastern horizon when the three men rode up the ridge toward the Cheyenne camp. The dew scent was thick in the air, reeking of pine and spruce, juniper, and fir. Partridges scurried through the underbrush ahead of them and jays squawked like angry fishwives, blue missiles flitting through the pine branches, leaving bouncing boughs in their wake. Overhead, a lone hawk sailed on a current of air, head moving back and forth, golden eyes scanning the game trails for prey beneath small puffs of cotton clouds.

Upwind, concealed in the trees, a man turned and headed up the ridge. He had been watching the white man and the two red men for a long time. He had read their hand signs, heard their words. He had made no sound. When he was far enough away, he began to run on moccasined feet. He was like a deer, fleet of foot, graceful, lithe, silent.

His name was Turtle.

26

Ollie Hobart rode into the renegade Cheyenne camp just at dawn, Army Mandrake and Rosa Delgado flanking him. Dick Tanner brought up the rear, riding several yards behind the others. He looked over his shoulder often, just to make sure no one was on their backtrail.

"No sentry," he said to Army. "Goddamned Injuns."

"I just hope they ain't drunk," Army said. "Blue Snake should have had sentries all around the camp, the bastard."

He looked at Rosa when he said it, and she fixed him with a scathing look. She had gotten sober the night before, but she knew both men no longer trusted her to stay away from the whiskey. Jubal Fry, no longer wearing an army uniform, rode beside her, his civilian clothes so new she could smell them. They reeked of cardboard and paper, store dust and mothballs.

Red Eagle stood outside his lean-to, smoking, when he saw Hobart and the others riding down from the ridge. Mist clung to the low spots around the camp, while clouds hugged the high peaks. There was no sunlight, only a soft pale glow to the east, beyond the craggy ridges and the tall pines rising above the foothills.

Blue Snake, in another lean-to, stepped out, rifle in hand. Other Cheyenne began to stir, emerging from their lean-tos, some rubbing their eyes, others wandering off into the trees to relieve themselves or drink at the stream that coursed through the camp. There were lean-tos scattered among the trees, their roofs covered with pine and spruce boughs, their upright poles unstripped, the bark still on, so that they blended in with their surroundings.

"You come," Red Eagle said to Hobart when he rode up.

Hobart swung out of the saddle without saying a word. Army glared down at Red Eagle and did not dismount.

Mist hung like smoke in the trees around the camp. A blue jay hopped around one of the lean-tos, chuckling in its throat. It cocked its head, then began pecking at a chunk of deadwood, seeking out a morning grub.

"Red Eagle," Mandrake said, "you got a sleepy camp here. No guards. We could have been soldiers riding up here."

"Me know you come. Scout come. Say he see you."

"What scout? I didn't see no scout," Army said.

Red Eagle looked over at a young brave who squatted by the brook, bony legs framing his bronze face. He spoke to the young brave, who stood up and walked over to Red Eagle.

"This one," Red Eagle said. "Him called Beaver. Good scout. He see. He come. He tell you come."

Beaver signed that he had seen Hobart's party ride up the canyon. Ollie was surprised that he could understand the "talking hands," as Mandrake had called this odd form of communication.

"Good," Ollie said, satisfied. "Now, call your men together. If you can understand me, I want you to tell them something. Do you understand?"

"Me hear. Me know you talk."

Ollie looked up at Mandrake.

"Does he understand what I'm saying, Army?"

"I think he does. I think he knows a lot more English than he lets on."

"Get off your horse. I want to get these . . . these men ready to attack those miners up the canyon."

Mandrake swung off his horse.

Red Eagle spoke to Beaver in the Cheyenne tongue. Beaver ran off to the other lean-tos and told all the men to come out and gather where the white faces stood.

Twenty Cheyenne came to listen to the white faces. Their clothes were tattered and patched, their shoes and moccasins worn, the sleeves of their shirts frayed at the cuffs, their trousers ill-fitting. Hobart looked them over, then turned to Red Eagle.

"I want you and your men to get their rifles and pistols. Bring all the ammunition you have. We are going to ride down to where the prospectors are and shoot every man jack there. Do you understand?"

"Me kill heap white faces," Red Eagle said. He pantomimed holding a rifle to his shoulder and made explosive sounds with his mouth. The Cheyenne gathered there grunted and uttered warlike oaths, speaking in their tongue and pantomiming taking scalps.

"Good," Hobart said. "Kill them all."

Mandrake made a sign with his hands.

"Heap die," Red Eagle said, grinning with a mouth full of carious teeth.

"And be quiet when we ride down there," Hobart said.

"I don't know that hand sign," Mandrake said to him.

Hobart walked up to Red Eagle, put a hand on his mouth, shook his head.

"Don't make a damned bit of noise. No talking," Hobart said.

"I know the sign for talking," Mandrake said.

Hobart removed his hand from Red Eagle's mouth. Red Eagle made the sign to his men, most of whom grunted in assent.

"Let's go," Hobart said.

Red Eagle held up a hand. None of the tribe moved. They all stood there, looking off across the ridge.

"What the hell?" Hobart said, his voice trailing off.

"Turtle come," Red Eagle said.

Blue Snake made a sign with his hands, two fingers held straight down, moving back and forth, like a man's legs.

Hobart looked where Red Eagle was looking. He didn't see anything. He didn't hear anything.

"I don't . . ." Hobart started to say.

"Here comes an Injun," Mandrake said, pointing. A man emerged from the trees. He was lean and lithe, wore moccasins, and carried a rifle in his hand. He had a pistol and holster strapped around his waist. His muslin shirt was clogged with dirt and there were fresh pine needles in his hair.

"Is that Turtle?" Hobart asked.

"Damned if I know," Mandrake said. "They all look pretty much alike to me, 'cept for Red Eagle and Blue Snake."

"Turtle heap good scout," Red Eagle said.

The clouds still hung low, but some of the mist was wafting off in gauzy tatters from the creek. Turtle stopped in front of Red Eagle. He did not seem winded at all, even though the air was thin at that altitude.

He spoke to Red Eagle, his speech full of hisses and tittering sounds. His hands moved slow and deliberately as he described what he had seen. Ollie watched him, fascinated, trying to decipher the sign language.

"You know what he's sayin', Army? With his hands, I mean."

"I see him measurin' distance and something about three men. Two redskins and a white man, near as I can figure."

"How long we going to be here?" Fry asked from a few feet away. "My butt's turning to wood just sitting here like this."

"Keep your shirt on, Fry," Ollie said. "Let's hear what this buck has to say."

Finally, Turtle stopped talking and his hands stopped moving. He walked to the creek, squatted down, scooped up water in his cupped hands, and drank with noisy slurps.

Red Eagle turned to Hobart.

"Turtle him say three men ride this way. One Lakota, one *Tsistsistas,* one white-face soldier. Soldier throw white-man clothes away. Him wear buckskins now. Him Ogallala. Lakota. Come to camp." He pointed to the ground.

Fry rode up, dismounted.

"He must be talking about Major Cresswell," Fry said. "He was captured by the Ogallaly Sioux when he was a boy. I think he robbed the armory with some renegade Cheyenne. But there was more than two Injuns got away with rifles and cartridges. He coming up here?"

"That's what Red Eagle said." Hobart shifted his weight. Mandrake could see that he was getting uneasy.

"I wonder where the other Cheyenne are," Fry said.

"Maybe Cresswell's comin' to join up with us," Mandrake said. "He's one of those I paid off to steal them rifles."

"Ask Red Eagle what he thinks," Hobart said to Mandrake. "Why is Cresswell comin' up here?"

"I'll try," Mandrake said.

From far away, they all heard the raucous screech of blue jays. The sound was faint, but it jarred the silence.

Red Eagle spoke to Blue Snake and then all of the other braves trotted to their lean-tos.

"Come quick," Red Eagle said.

"Is this white man going to fight with us?" Ollie said. "You savvy?"

"Me savvy. No. White face want braves go with him. North." He made a sign with one arm, pointing north. "Many brave. Heap guns. North."

"I don't like it," Ollie said to Mandrake. "Get those horses out of sight. Rosa, take cover. Dick, you and Fry come with Army and me."

"What are you goin' to do, Ollie?" Mandrake said.

"We'll just find out what that damned turncoat Cresswell is doin' up here. He stole rifles meant for this bunch and those missing Injuns. I don't like it none. The bastard."

He turned to Red Eagle.

"Keep all your bucks in the trees, Red Eagle," he said. "Out of sight. Savvy?"

To his surprise, Ollie was using his hands, gesturing toward the trees.

Fry started leading his horse toward the trees. Rosa and Tanner rode up and followed Army and Ollie to a hiding place among the pines and spruce.

The jays down the ridge grew louder with their invective. Soon, the clearing was empty. Ollie stood next to a pine, his rifle in hand, the muzzle pointing to the ground.

Mandrake hunkered down behind a juniper bush a few feet away. He jacked a cartridge into the chamber of his Winchester. Fry drew his pistol. Rosa sat down, a pine at her back. Dick Tanner came back from tying up the horses and took a position behind a small fir tree, his rifle at the ready.

"Damn," Ollie muttered to Mandrake. "How far up the canyon are them prospectors? Will they hear us if we shoot?"

"About two miles, I reckon. But the canyon twists some. They might not hear a shot or two."

"Shit," said Ollie.

The gold wasn't going to go anywhere, he knew. But he was thirsting for blood. And he didn't like being double-crossed by that damned Cresswell.

He felt the blood pulse in his neck as his anger swelled within him. He fingered the trigger of his rifle, sighted it as he held the barrel against the tree.

Maybe, he thought, *I won't even give that bastard Cresswell the benefit of the doubt.*

He smiled.

He was beginning to feel better already.

27

John descended the trail, which coursed the side of the ridge at an angle. Ben rode right behind him, followed by Herzog and the two sergeants.

He had seen a number of such trails along the ridge, but this one led straight down to the canyon floor, while the others had strayed off in all directions like a spider's web.

Just beyond the trail he had seen a high bluff, rimrock, and knew this would be the easiest path. They had made good time and had seen nothing on the opposite ridge: no riders, no sign of Cresswell and what he figured were two Indians.

"Game trail?" he asked Herzog when they reached the canyon floor.

"Sheep trail. Basque sheepherders used to graze their sheep up here in the summers. They stopped coming here when they saw the dead horses."

"Dead horses?"

"Just up ahead. The bones are still there."

They rode up the canyon. Just below the massive rock outcropping, the sheer bluff that resembled some ancient architectural structure, the ground was littered with bones and horse skulls. John looked up to the top of the sheer bluff.

"They fell from up there?" John asked Herzog.

"I guess so. Legend says a bunch of Utes rode up here, chased by Arapahos. When they were cornered and knew they were going to die, the Utes supposedly jumped their horses off that cliff."

"Christ," Ben exclaimed.

John examined the bones more closely. There were human skulls mingled with the horse bones. He shuddered. All of the human skulls had been smashed. There were large holes in the top such as might have been made by a stone war club or a rock. Some of the horse skulls showed signs of having once been painted. There were faded symbols, colored red and green and blue. John wondered if the Arapaho had ridden down to make sure the Utes were all dead and maybe take their scalps for proof and for bragging. And maybe they had painted the story on the horse skulls, daubed on pictographs for their enemies to read.

"It's only a legend," Herzog said. "Happened a long time ago. Look at how bleached all those bones are."

"Let's get the hell out of here," Ben said. "How far is it to that mining camp, Lieutenant?"

"Couple of miles. Canyon twists a lot from here on in, so it's hard to tell. Used to be a river run down here, but the Basques dammed it off to form a lake up top. Now there's just seepage when it rains or the snow melts in the spring."

"This place gives me the creepy crawlies," Ben said. "Any chance of that dam breakin' while we're ridin' up it?"

Herzog laughed and looked at Sergeant Will Crisp.

"I been up there," Crisp said. "That dam is solid rock and dirt and the beavers did what the dynamiters might have missed. That dam ain't never goin' to break, less'n there be a quake. Ain't that right, Daryl?"

Freeman nodded. "Big old lake up there, like it's in a hole. Looks mighty deep and green as jade when the sun's just right. Me 'n Will wanted to take a swim there when we rode up, but you get in it, you ain't getting out."

"That makes these old bones feel a lot

better," Ben said.

John was silent, studying the trail up the canyon. It was rutted with wagon tracks, but there had been no water to soften the soil since spring, he figured. The horse and wagon tracks were at least three weeks old. The miners must be about ready to go into Fort Laramie for supplies in a week or so.

"Rolf," he said, "do they have a head man up there at the camp? Somebody I can talk to?"

"Kind of," Herzog said. "Several of them come to the fort fairly often, wanting one thing or another, besides grub and tools. One of them seems to speak for the bunch. A man named Luther Randolph."

"Know him pretty well, do you?" John asked.

"Pretty well. I've had dealings with him. Fact is, he's about the only one who does any talking. These prospectors are a tight-lipped bunch. They don't say much."

"Think I could get along with him?" John asked, looking up at the right ridge every so often. The canyon took a sharp twist to the left and he stared ahead. He saw that the trail was even more crooked. From the exposed rocks, he could see signs that raging rivers had once coursed down the canyon. The water had eaten away at the rock and soil and there were stones and boulders lining both sides of the trail. The canyon was wide enough, however, so that it might not fill up for hundreds of years.

"Yeah, I think you and Luther would get along. You don't talk much, either, and from what I hear, you know a little something about prospecting. Fact is, Randolph may have heard of you."

"Oh? Why so?" John asked.

"The news of that massacre down in Colorado got way up here. Randolph asked Ward a lot of questions, knowing the colonel's son was one of those who got killed. You ever heard of Luther Randolph, you or Ben?"

"Not me," Ben said.

"No," John said. "I never heard his name before. Where's he from?"

"That's something you're not likely to find out from any of the miners up here. Like I said, they're a tight-lipped bunch."

"So were we," Ben said. "Sure as hell didn't help much."

"With no river running here, these must be hard-rock miners," John said to Herzog.

"Yeah. They buy a lot of lumber and dynamite, blasting caps. I asked Luther once if they had stumbled onto the mother lode."

"What did he say?" John asked.

"He just laughed. Didn't really answer me."

Just then, they heard a muffled explosion. Then it was quiet. John figured it came from at least two miles away.

"Must be deep into it," Ben said. "And they probably used a half stick."

Herzog looked at him, partly in surprise, partly in admiration.

"Sounds right," John said.

They were met at the edge of the settlement by two men carrying rifles.

"Halt," one of them shouted.

John reined up. So did the others.

"Who be ye?" said the other man.

"Friends," Herzog replied. "We came to talk to Luther. I'm Lieutenant Herzog from Fort Laramie."

"Well, why didn't you say so, Lieutenant. Who you got with ye?" said the first man.

"Miners from the massacre in Colorado," Herzog said, thinking fast.

Dust hung in the air from the blast deep in the mine. It had taken a long time to make its way from the shaft out into the air.

The first man waved them on and Herzog waved to both men as they passed.

Ben was taking it all in, gazing at the scaffolding that had been erected on the side of one tall ridge. Broken rocks lay everywhere, talus was strewn along the base of the mountain; shale and iron-streaked rocks lay in jumbled piles, as well. He saw wheelbarrows and pickaxes, coiled ropes, tents, cooking irons, pots and pans, kegs of nails, boxes of dynamite under small lean-tos. Men looked up from their dry rockers. Some stood with picks or shovels in their hands. A couple were smoking pipes, another a cigarette. A few of the men wore no shirts. Others wore grimy shirts, ragged, patched trousers, battered, crumpled hats. Horses and mules were in separate pole corrals. Smoke rose from a fire over which hung a blackened kettle.

"They got 'em some digs here, all right," Ben said, his voice almost a whisper. "Kind of gets your blood workin', don't it, Johnny?"

"Brings back some memories, all right," John said.

"Hello the camp," Herzog called, cupping both hands around his mouth. "Luther, you here?"

"He's right over yonder," one of the men said, pointing to a big, brawny man who was working a dry rocker next to the old streambed. He and another man set the rocker down and stood up.

"Rolf? That you?" Randolph yelled.

"Want to talk to you, Luther. Have you meet a couple of friends."

"Well, light down, all of you," Randolph said, walking over to them. "We done et our breakfast vittles, but we can scare up some coffee. Pot's always on."

Rolf introduced Ben and John to Randolph, explained who they were and why they were there.

"We might not have much time," John said. "Can you have your men grab rifles and pistols and listen to what I have to say?"

"There going to be a fight?" Luther said.

"I think a bunch of renegade Cheyenne and some of the men who killed my family and our friends are going to swarm all over here to try and steal your gold."

"Hell, it's all pretty much ore. Assays out pretty good, though."

"Can you and your men defend themselves? We might be going up against twenty or thirty rifles," John said.

"Oh, we can give a good account of ourselves, I reckon." Randolph whistled and all of the men stood up and some started walking their way. Some heads peeked out of the mines above them. Two men were walking down from the dam, carrying wooden pails full of water.

John sized Randolph up. He was a rugged-looking man with a florid face, a full beard, grime rings around his neck, arms that were all sinew, muscle, and hard bone.

"I'll strap on my Colt Walker and grab my rifle," Randolph said. To the man next to him, he said, "Kelly, tell everybody to grab a rifle and strap on their pistols. We might be fightin' off Injuns."

"Right, Luther," Kelly said and started running toward the nearest men, yelling at the top of his lungs.

"Be back in a minute," Randolph said.

Men began to stream back down to where John, Ben, Herzog, Freeman, and Crisp were. Many of them started asking questions all at once.

"What's this about a fight?" asked one burly man with a belly dripping over his belt. He had about six teeth in his head and no neck.

"We got Injuns?" another asked, panting from running about an eighth of a mile to join the assemblage.

"Men, this is John Savage," Herzog said. "He's in charge. He'll tell you what to do."

"You the Savage from down Coloraddy way?" a man asked.

"He is," Ben said, "and I'm Ben Russell. The same men who shot up our camp and kilt near about all of us are comin' down here to do the same to you, if they can."

"Be damned if they will," another man said, a belligerent look on his face.

Randolph rejoined them. He had his Walker holstered and hanging from his belt. He carried a Winchester and was stuffing cartridges in his pocket. He had put on a shirt, but had not tucked it in.

Just then, they all heard something that turned them all to stone. Around the bend, they heard hoofbeats and war cries. Then the sound of rifles cracking like bullwhips.

John thought of the two guards. He wondered if they'd had time to take cover, or if they had been surprised and shot dead.

Then there was no longer time to think. He saw dust rise in the air down canyon, and then saw the first horses round the bend. Indians brandished rifles and their screams shot needles of ice into the back of his neck.

"Take cover," Herzog shouted and slapped his horse on the rump.

John jerked his Winchester from its scabbard and worked the lever, jacking a cartridge into the firing chamber. Ben pulled his rifle from its sheath and batted his and John's horses on the rumps.

There was no time to look for cover. John

sank to one knee and put his rifle to his shoulder. He drew a bead on the nearest Cheyenne while rifles exploded all around him.

"Come on, Hobart," John breathed as he squeezed the trigger. "Just show your damned face."

And then, they were all enveloped in a cloud of dust as horses streamed up the canyon at full gallop. The Cheyenne fanned out, hugged the flanks of their horses so that they were poor targets.

A miner screamed and crashed to the ground, a hole in his throat gushing blood.

John took aim at a Cheyenne riding straight toward him and fired a shot. He saw the Cheyenne grab his chest as the bullet ripped into his breastbone. He raised his arms and his rifle sailed through the air. He tumbled from his horse and a Cheyenne behind him danced his horse around him with all the skill of a trick rider.

Men screamed and the Cheyenne yelled their bloodcurdling war cries. There was a cloud of dust and orange flames, the whistle and whine of bullets sizzling through the air and caroming off rocks.

But all John Savage could think of was Ollie Hobart.

Where in hell are you, Ollie, he thought, as

he levered another cartridge into the chamber of his Winchester. He swung his rifle, looking for another target.

The smell of fresh blood filled his nostrils. His heart pumped fast. And he saw again, in a corner of his mind, Hobart and his men riding into camp, their guns blazing. Only here, in this dry canyon, he couldn't see a damned thing for all the reddish dust and cloud-white smoke.

28

Sunrise spread into the canyon, lighting the dust and smoke. As if part of the weather conspiracy, great white clouds billowed up from the other side of the lake and spilled over the canyon in a muscular show of strength. The snowy thunderheads awoke the sleeping wind. Gusts poured down in the canyon, blowing away the smoke, swirling out the dust, bringing the battlefield into stark relief.

John saw the man charging straight toward him. No mistaking the clothing and the horse. A few feet away, Herzog saw the man, too, and looked over at John.

"That Hobart?" Herzog said.

John did not answer. He dropped the front blade sight onto the man's chest, lined it up with the rear slot. He waited until Hobart was thirty feet away. He didn't see a gun in his hands, but Hobart hunched over, gripping the saddle horn. Now there was only his hat and the small hump of his back for a target.

John held his breath, dropped the sight to the horse's chest, and squeezed the trigger. The horse stumbled, blood gushing from its blasted pectoral muscles. Its front legs folded and the man in the saddle straightened up. John levered another shell into the chamber, found the man's body in his sights, and squeezed the trigger.

Blood spurted from a hole in the man's belly. The horse collapsed and skidded to a stop less than ten yards away. The man hurtled over its head and landed near John and Herzog, flat on his back.

"Buckskins," the man said.

"That's not Hobart," Herzog told John.

John looked at the man's face. He had never seen him before.

But he knew it wasn't Hobart.

"Damn," he said.

"That's Major Cresswell."

Cresswell was dressed in Hobart's clothes and had been riding his horse.

"Buckskins," Cresswell said again, gasping for air, sucking it into his blood-clotted throat.

John levered the Winchester. The empty hull ejected. The chamber was empty. John laid the rifle down, started patting his pockets for more cartridges.

"Look out," Herzog shouted at John.

Out of the corner of his eye, Savage saw a man in buckskins riding toward him, a rifle pointing. John drew his pistol and rolled to his side. Herzog fired at the man's horse, an army horse. His bullet struck the horse in the belly and the animal buckled.

"That's Hobart," John said and scrambled to his feet.

Hobart got off a shot, but it went wild. The next minute, he was afoot. His rifle butt struck the saddle horn and the energy wrested it from his hands. He landed on his feet and clawed for his pistol, drawing it from his holster, cocking on the rise.

"You sonofabitch," Hobart spat, raising his arm to aim the pistol at John.

John went into a crouch and fired at Hobart. He hit the hammer with the butt of his left hand, bringing it to full cock, and fired again just as Hobart squeezed the trigger of his own pistol.

John's first bullet caught Hobart in the ribs just above the left side of his diaphragm. The second slammed into his chest just above the first hole, smashing ribs and lungs into pulp with the force of a hurricane. Hobart's legs went out from under him and he crumpled to the ground in a heap, blood gushing from two holes in his torso with every beat of his heart.

The miners gave a cheer as the few remaining Cheyenne turned tail and raced their horses back down the canyon.

"Don't shoot," someone cried, and Rosa emerged from the dust cloud on foot, her face and clothes covered with dust.

"It's a damned woman," yelled Luther. "A Mex."

Rosa saw Hobart lying there. John stood over him, smoke curling from the barrel of his pistol.

"Did you kill him?" she said to John.

"He's dying, Rosa."

"You bastard," she said, and a pistol appeared in her right hand as if by magic.

John heard the snick of the hammer as she cocked it.

Ben, out of rifle ammunition, started to reach for his pistol. The battleground turned suddenly quiet.

Everyone stared at Rosa as she kept walking toward John, aiming her pistol at him.

"You're just as bad as Hobart," John said. "Cut from the same bolt of cloth."

Then he fired, aiming straight at Rosa's head. The bullet smashed her right between the eyes. Her eyes went cloudy, glazed over, and she crumpled into a heap, her mouth gaping, her eyes closed.

John heard a loud gasp from several of the miners.

"He done shot a woman," a man muttered.

"Aw, it was a Mex," said another.

Herzog put a hand on John's back.

"Good shooting," he said. "You got your revenge."

"It wasn't for revenge," John said. "It was for my father and mother, my kid sister, and all of my friends Hobart murdered."

"Looky, John," Ben said, running up to Herzog and John. "I got that bastard Mandrake, and Luther here, he put old Dick Tanner's lights out. Damn, we got 'em all, ever' damned one of them."

John felt his knees go weak. Inside, he was shaking like the yellow leaves of an aspen. He drew in a breath, lifted his pistol so that the sun glistened off the silver filigree, the legend scrolled on its blued barrel.

The clouds enveloped the canyon where the dead lay. Hobart gave out a last gasp and his eyes glazed over with the frost of death. A shadow fell over the quick and the dead.

"It's over, John," Ben said, putting an arm on John's shoulder. "Finally. We got 'em all. You done good."

Was it over? John wondered. Were there other men like Hobart wandering the earth, robbing and killing, with no regard for human life? He did not know.

And he hoped he never would.

We hope you have enjoyed this Large Print book. Other Thorndike, Wheeler, and Chivers Press Large Print books are available at your library or directly from the publishers.

For information about current and upcoming titles, please call or write, without obligation, to:

Publisher
Thorndike Press
295 Kennedy Memorial Drive
Waterville, ME 04901
Tel. (800) 223-1244

or visit our Web site at:

http://gale.cengage.com/thorndike

OR

Chivers Large Print
published by BBC Audiobooks Ltd
St James House, The Square
Lower Bristol Road
Bath BA2 3SB
England
Tel. +44(0) 800 136919
email: bbcaudiobooks@bbc.co.uk
www.bbcaudiobooks.co.uk

All our Large Print titles are designed for easy reading, and all our books are made to last.